THE PUFFIN TREASURY OF
AUSTRALIAN
CHILDREN'S STORIES

VIKING/PUFFIN

Penguin Books Australia Ltd
487 Maroondah Highway, PO Box 257
Ringwood, Victoria 3134, Australia
Penguin Books Ltd
Harmondsworth, Middlesex, England
Viking Penguin, A Division of Penguin Books USA Inc.
375 Hudson Street, New York, New York 10014, USA
Penguin Books Canada Limited
10 Alcorn Avenue, Toronto, Ontario, Canada, M4V 3B2
Penguin Books (N.Z.) Ltd
Cnr Rosedale and Airborne Roads, Albany, Auckland, New Zealand

First published by Penguin Books Australia, 1997

1 3 5 7 9 10 8 6 4 2

Stories selected and introduced by Kay Ronai

Typeset in 14/20pt Bembo by Midland Typesetters, Maryborough, Victoria
Produced by The Australian Book Connection
Bound by M & M Binders

National Library of Australia
Cataloguing-in-Publication data:

The Puffin treasury of Australian children's stories.

ISBN 0 670 87868 5.
1. Children's stories, Australian.
A823.30809282

THE PUFFIN TREASURY OF
AUSTRALIAN
CHILDREN'S STORIES

Puffin Books

CONTENTS

∾

INTRODUCTION

∽

A book.
There are no gimmicks, no buttons to press, no controls to conquer, no joystick to juggle, no noise… There are just words. And you. And your imagination.

The Puffin Treasury of Australian Children's Stories is no ordinary book - if a book can ever be called ordinary. You will meet giants and vampires, ordinary people and talking animals. Some of these characters live in fantastic worlds of talking gumnuts, dastardly pudding-thieves or flying pigs. Some find themselves thrust into overwhelming situations - whether it be fleeing from war-torn Sarajevo or slimy, slithering slobberers, having to conquer a formidable opponent or being adrift on a perilous sea. Others must cope with everyday dilemmas - such as being invited to the class nerd's birthday party, or sitting next to someone they hate.

What would *you* do if you found your bum was missing one morning so your pyjama pants fell down, or that there was a wolf outside your door, or you discovered a helpless, orphaned pelican? Through books *you* can become explorer, adviser, observer, and friend – at any time, anywhere, at your own pace.

The Puffin Treasury of Australian Children's Stories shows Australian writing at its liveliest, with exciting excerpts, poems and complete stories from many of our most popular authors, including Allan Baillie, Graeme Base, Max Fatchen, Morris Gleitzman, Paul Jennings, Victor Kelleher, Robin Klein, Caroline Macdonald, Ruth Park, Emily Rodda, Gillian Rubinstein, Jenny Wagner, Tim Winton and Patricia Wrightson.

As you browse through this book you will also find illustrations by some of Australia's best artists including Ron Brooks, Vivienne Goodman, Robert Ingpen, Sally Morgan, Betina Ogden, Craig Smith and Jane Tanner. Most illustrations are from the original books, while some have been drawn especially for this treasury.

From the reassuring classics such as the irreverent *The Magic Pudding*, *The Muddle-headed Wombat* and *Snugglepot and Cuddlepie* to the very latest in spookiness from Paul Jennings and Morris Gleitzman, there is something for everyone. New worlds to explore, new friends to encounter, new dramas to resolve. And hours and hours of enjoyment.

Happy reading.

Paul Jennings

THE CABBAGE PATCH FIB

ILLUSTRATED BY CRAIG SMITH

Confused about where babies come from? Read on!

MY brother Chris is only eight years old, which is rather young to have a baby. Well, 'have a baby' is probably not quite the right way to put it, but there was a baby and it sure thought Chris was its father. He was in charge of it, that's for certain. Anyway, I had better start at the beginning so you know the whole story. If you don't believe it I don't blame you – but it's true.

It all started at tea time. The whole eight of us – six kids and Mum and Dad – were eating spaghetti. We kids were all killing ourselves laughing because Chris (who can be a real pain at times) had put a piece of spaghetti up his nose and left one end hanging out over his lip so that it looked like something I would rather not talk about. It was a grotty thing to do but it really did look funny and we couldn't help cracking up.

Dad hadn't noticed because he was too busy pretending not to be watching *Doctor Who* on the TV. It is a rule in our family that the TV is not on at tea time but somehow or other Dad never notices it is on until *Doctor Who* is over.

Suddenly Dad saw the piece of spaghetti and he began to throw a wobbly. 'Take that disgusting thing out of your nose,' he roared at Chris. 'You are a hopeless child.'

Dad started to go purple. Then he began banging his head up and down on the table next to his plate. 'What did I do to deserve this?' he moaned. 'First the boy puts a length of spaghetti up his

nose and then when I ask him to remove it he sucks it in his mouth and swallows it. Doesn't anyone in this family have any table manners at all?' We all tried hard not to laugh but giggles kept breaking out.

On the TV I saw Doctor Who was just about to be eaten by a green, two-headed monster. The funny music came on which meant you had to wait until tomorrow to find out what happened. I knew Doctor Who would not be eaten alive. He never is because he has to be around for the next episode. Anyway, now that the show was over Dad got up and switched it off. 'That's it,' he yelled. 'From now on there is no TV at tea time. We are having good manners and proper conversation for a change.'

He says this about once a week but it never lasts more than one or two days, so we were not too worried.

'I want a proper discussion,' Dad went on. 'Intelligent conversation about important things you do at school. Like who made the moon or where flies go in winter. Who has a topic for discussion?'

There was a long silence and then Chris said, 'Where do babies come from, Dad?'

Dad started to go red. He was not expecting this one. 'Well,' he said. 'Um, er, well, it's like this, er, you see, Chris, well, er … they come from, from, er … the cabbage patch. Yes, they come from the cabbage patch.'

Mum was looking at Dad in a funny way. She didn't like it because Dad was not telling Chris the truth. Everyone knew that it was a fib except Chris. He looked interested.

'How do they get there?' he asked.

'They grow out of the cabbages. Yes, they grow out of the cabbages at night,' Dad said weakly.

'Wow,' responded Chris. 'There could be a new kid arrive tonight, couldn't there?'

Everyone was looking daggers at Dad but he just said, 'You never know – we could just be that unlucky.' Then he got up and switched on the news, which meant we had to do the washing up. It's not fair how parents make their kids do all the work while they watch the news but that is the way it always is – even on days when they are not trying to get out of answering a difficult question.

Well, the rest of the evening passed as normal and no more was said about babies. Finally I went to bed and was just starting to fall off to sleep when I heard Chris get up. We share a room and he sleeps on the bunk above me.

He climbed out of bed and got dressed. Then he took his torch out of the top drawer of the dressing table.

I heard him leave the bedroom and then I heard a 'click' as the back door closed. He had gone outside. I quickly put on my track suit and followed him out into the back yard.

Everything outside was dark and at first I couldn't see where Chris had gone. Then I noticed the torch flashing right at the bottom of the garden in the vegetable patch.

I made my way down to Chris as quietly as I could, but he heard me coming and looked up from where he was rummaging about among the cabbages.

I called out to him through the darkness, 'What do you think you are doing?'

'Looking for babies,' he said. 'Dad reckons that one could be sprouting tonight. We can't just leave it out here until morning. It might catch a cold and die.'

'Oh, no,' I said. 'You don't believe that load of codswallop, do you? Babies don't come out of cabbage patches, they grow inside their mother.'

A look of disbelief came over his face. 'Where?' he asked. 'Whereabouts in their mother?'

'Here,' I said, rubbing my stomach. 'Somewhere in here.'

'Don't give me that,' he said. 'Pull the other one. That's where all the potato and sausage and gravy and custard go. You couldn't have a baby mixed up with that lot. Ugh. The poor thing. You don't have to hide it from me. I'm old enough to know the truth about babies growing in the cabbage patch.'

He wouldn't listen to me any more. He just kept on searching under the cabbages. 'Help me look,' he said. 'One might have crawled over there into the potatoes.'

I decided to humour him and pretended to be searching for a baby amongst the vegetables. After a while I heard him say, 'Got one.'

'Got what?' I asked.

'A baby, of course,' he replied.

'Great,' I said, making out I believed him. He certainly had a good imagination.

'Keep looking,' he ordered. 'There might be another one. It might be twins.'

I started to laugh quietly to myself but quickly stopped. I heard something that made my hair stand on end. It was a baby crying.

Sally Morgan

THE FLYING EMU

ILLUSTRATED BY THE AUTHOR

EMU was once the most colourful bird in Australia. His head feathers were brilliant blue, his huge wings were shades of pink and purple, his body was like spun gold, and his big feet were bright red with lime-green claws. While some of the other birds thought Emu was a bit much, Emu loved himself.

'I'm so handsome!' he sighed as he gazed at his reflection in the still waters of the billabong. He leant down closer to the surface and burst into song:

I love my rainbow feathers,
I love my great, big wings,
I love the way my eyes shine,
I'm a wonderful handsome thing!

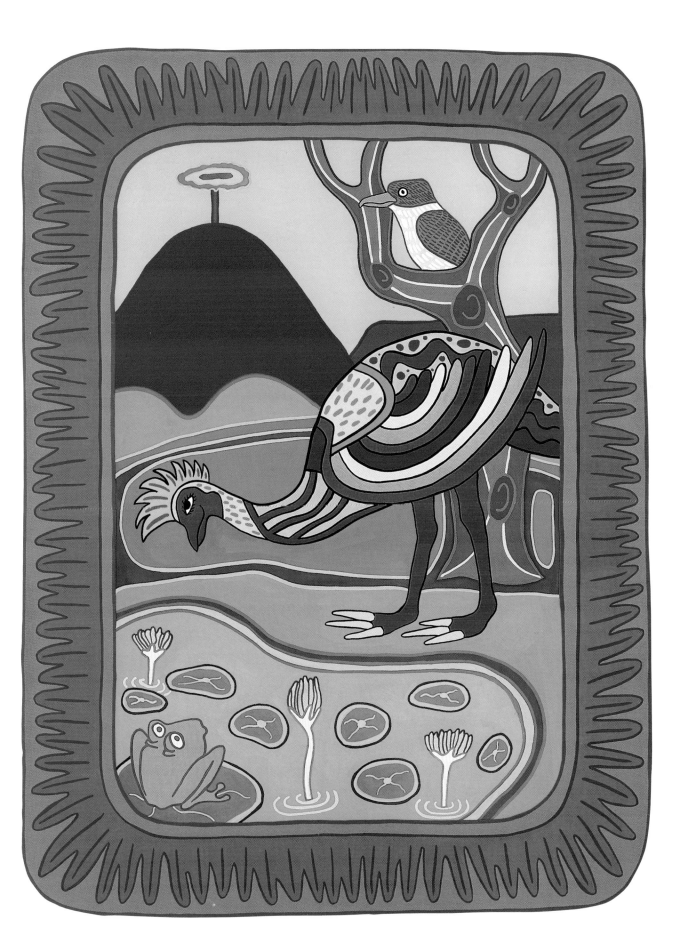

Then he pursed his beak and made a long, drawn-out kissing sound.

Frog surfaced suddenly in the middle of Emu's reflection and croaked, 'Emu old buddy, how are you today?' Frog was a great admirer of Emu and had been trying to make friends with him for a long time.

'Buzz off, Froggy,' Emu hissed. 'You're spoiling my view!'

Frog felt quite hurt at that. 'Don't you want any friends?' he asked.

Emu laughed nastily. 'Why would I want friends when I have myself?' he sneered. This made Frog feel very sad so he dived back under the water.

Now Kookaburra, a bird known for his mocking laugh, was watching from a nearby tree. He was very jealous of Emu and had been planning a way to get rid of him for a long time.

'Now is the perfect moment to put my little plan into action,' he muttered to himself. He called out loudly, 'You're quite right, Emu – Frog is as dull as mud. Whereas your brilliance can only be compared to the shining noonday sun!'

Emu kept staring at his own reflection, but just for a moment he smiled encouragingly at Kookaburra. Emu loved compliments.

'Your wings are like twin rainbows,' continued Kookaburra. 'Your head is a sparkling sapphire and your feet are radiant rubies.'

Emu nodded proudly. It was all true.

'I'm so dull,' Kookaburra sighed sadly. 'When I sing everyone thinks I'm laughing at them.'

Emu nodded in agreement. He didn't think much of Kookaburra either. He smiled contentedly at his own reflection again and once more burst into song:

What a wonderful bird I am!
What a wonderful bird I am!
Forget the rest 'cause I'm the best!
Yes, I'm the handsomest.

Kookaburra felt sickened by Emu's vanity, but he managed to say smoothly, 'What a tune, what a voice.'

Emu chuckled smugly. Really, there was no end to his talents.

'I'll never be as glorious as you,' sighed Kookaburra sadly. 'Thank heaven I can fly fast and high, otherwise I'd have nothing at all to boast about.'

Emu tilted his head and asked curiously, 'Are you saying I can't fly fast and high?'

'Of course not!' replied Kookaburra. 'It's just that I'm so small compared with you. I don't have a giant body or giant feet to weigh me down.'

Emu looked at his feet. They were big. But then, he reasoned, a magnificent body needed magnificent feet and legs to carry it.

While Emu continued to gaze adoringly at his feet, Kookaburra squashed a laugh. His plan was working well and he didn't want to spoil it by laughing out of turn.

'Feet aren't really important,' he said as he interrupted Emu's thoughts. 'Wings are the main thing.'

Emu nodded and puffed out his chest. Then, in a moment of great pride, he spread out his glorious wings to their full span.

'Oh marvellous, marvellous!' admired Kookaburra. 'What an honour to see such a sight.' He spread out his own small brown and white wings, but Emu laughed nastily and said, 'I wouldn't bother if I were you.'

Kookaburra quickly pulled his wings in and said, 'I know my wings aren't twin rainbows, but I *can* fly fast and high. I could even fly to the sun if I wanted to.'

'Fly to the sun,' Emu scoffed. 'You're not only dull but stupid too!'

'You can insult me as much as you like,' taunted Kookaburra, 'but that won't change the fact that while my wings are small and light, yours are big and heavy. It's only logical that I must be able to fly faster and higher than you.'

Emu was outraged. What a nasty, horrible little bird Kookaburra was.

'You haven't got a brain in your head!' hissed Emu angrily.

'That may be so,' said Kookaburra, 'but that still doesn't mean you can fly to the sun. You're just too big and fat!'

'I am not!' screeched Emu. 'I can beat you at anything, any day, any time. I challenge you to a flying contest tomorrow at dawn.'

Kookaburra shook his head. 'No good,' he said. 'I will only accept your challenge if we fly at noon. That way everyone can see me win. And I want to go first!'

'Oh no you're not!' objected Emu. 'It's my challenge so I'll go first. Noon it is!'

Kookaburra was so excited that Emu had fallen so easily into his trap that he couldn't help emitting a small, mocking laugh, 'Haa, haa . . .'

'What was that?' asked Emu suspiciously.

'Aah, aah . . . nothing. I was just clearing my throat.'

Emu sent him a withering glance and then returned to looking at himself in the billabong.

Kookaburra, feeling very pleased with himself, flew off to find a resting place for the night. The sun was just beginning to set, and he wanted to have a good sleep so he could enjoy the next day.

'Oh yes,' he chuckled to himself, 'the sun is not only brightest at noonday, but hottest too. I am going to have fun with Emu.'

Towards noon the next day all the bush creatures gathered at the billabong to see who would win this unusual challenge. Emu hadn't had such a large audience for ages. He pranced, preened and strutted through the crowd. Now and then he spread out his extraordinary wings for show. And in moments of silence he burst into song about himself.

'Poor Kookaburra,' sighed Kangaroo, who was the official starter. 'He hasn't got a chance. I almost wish he could win, just to teach Emu a lesson.'

When the sun stood directly over the tallest tree on a nearby hill, Emu knew it was time to begin.

He turned to Kookaburra and said unpleasantly, 'If I were you I'd never fly again after I'm done!'

'After you're done . . .' retorted Kookaburra, but his voice trailed away. He wanted to say, 'You'll be done, all right – well done!' But he didn't. Instead he hung his head and feigned sadness.

'Just ignore him, Kookaburra,' said Wombat, who was a friendly creature.

Emu raised one big foot over Wombat, who scurried away.

'Are you ready, Emu?' asked Kangaroo.

'Of course I am!'

'Right, stand back everyone,' commanded Kangaroo.

Emu strutted to the starting line.

'On your mark.'

Emu dug in his claws and leant forward.

'Get ready.'

Emu breathed deeply and puffed out his chest.

'Go!'

Emu was off, taking great strides down past the billabong and into a clearing. His huge wings spread out, his feet and legs disappeared under him, and he was away.

Soon he was no more than a small, dark speck on the wide horizon. A speck that gradually grew smaller and smaller as it moved towards the sun. It wasn't long before he'd disappeared completely.

'Ooh!' they all gasped when a small, bright red ball suddenly exploded and shot out from the surface of the sun.

'What's happening?' asked Wombat.

No one bothered to reply. They were all too busy running for cover as the flaming crimson ball grew larger and larger and plummeted towards Earth.

The whistling sound the ball made grew louder and louder until suddenly there was a huge splash. The ball had landed in the billabong. Steam hissed and billowed everywhere. Once the bush creatures had stopped coughing they all began to creep out from behind their separate hiding places. Kangaroo bravely led the way back to the billabong.

'Argh!' they all screamed in horror when a strange-looking head on a long, thin neck popped up out of the water.

'Is . . . is . . . is that you, Emu?' asked Wombat nervously. Then he began to chuckle at what he thought was his foolishness. Of course it wasn't Emu. Emu didn't look anything like that.

But Kookaburra, realising what had happened, began to laugh and laugh.

The mud-coloured monster with the strange head and long neck stood up, shook himself and walked from the water. He glared disgustedly at Kookaburra, who was practically hysterical, and said, 'Yes, it is me. I am Emu.'

There was stunned silence.

'But where are your beautiful feathers?' croaked Frog.

'Burnt,' choked Emu.

'What about your wings?'

'They exploded when I reached the sun. All I have left now are these small, brown stumps. I don't think I will be able to fly any more. It looks like you've got the last laugh after all, Kookaburra,' finished Emu tearfully.

Everyone looked accusingly at Kookaburra. Emu had been terribly vain, but he didn't deserve this.

Kookaburra didn't feel the tiniest bit guilty. He congratulated himself on having the last laugh as he flew off into the bush cackling, 'Kook, kook, koo, kaa, kaa, haa, haa, haa . . .'

When the water in the billabong finally settled and Emu was able to have a good look at his new appearance, he was so embarrassed that he ran away as fast as his legs could carry him.

For days and days he ran. For weeks and weeks he ran. He

ran so much that he became very, very good at it. Soon he was the fastest-running bird in Australia. And it wasn't long before he was singing a new song:

> I love my great big feet!
> I love my strong, fast legs!
> I run so fast, you eat my dust,
> I'm the fastest bird around!

Max Fatchen

THE RAILWAY HISTORICAL STEAM WEEKEND

ILLUSTRATED BY MICHAEL ATCHISON

'WILL you come,' says the letter, 'and join
our outing.
Meal provided and time to spend
Along a line that is rarely travelled
For the railway historical steam weekend.'

The guard is dressed in his railway splendour,
With buttons and braid in a beautiful blend.
The engine's green, with a shining tender
For the railway historical steam weekend.

We stare at the signals old and ailing,
Our carriages labelled with their class.
The luggage rack has a real brass railing
And larks awake in the railyard grass.

The cows go galloping, tails uplifted,
The carriages sway with a rackety beat.
A banner of smoke on the fields has drifted.
It's my turn now for the window seat.

There's a leather smell from the green seat covers.
The woodwork moves in a creaking song,
With corridors full of railway lovers
All pushing about where they don't belong.

My father's loaded with information
On regulations and rules and Acts
And pages and pages on varying gauges
And funnels and tunnels and railway facts.

My father explains that it's quite improper
For mother to think he has wheels for brains
Describing expresses, the slow goods stopper,
But adults go mad when they play at trains.

So he looks at his watch as our time grows shorter,
Announcing the stations along our run.
He's wearing a cap with the title 'Porter'
For he likes to join in the railway fun.

We huff through cuttings with old rockfaces
And clatter on bridges above slow creeks
To all the mysterious railway places,
With a coal-black smudge on our wind-whipped cheeks.

We visit the engine at one small siding,
It hisses and pants like an iron god.
The driver is peering and prodding at pistons
And poking the great connecting rod.

Then on again with the white steam spouting
While signals dip near the journey's end.
My father says what a splendid outing,
A most educational steam weekend ...

Well-organised and a worthwhile function,
With smoky wind and the rocking bend.
(But I liked tea at the local junction
On the railway historical steam weekend.)

Norman Lindsay

THE MAGIC PUDDING

ILLUSTRATED BY THE AUTHOR

After the previous day's events, Sam Sawnoff, Bill Barnacle and Bunyip Bluegum are desperate to protect their Puddin' from the treacherous puddin'-thieves.

THE most annoying part of it all was that when the puddin'-thieves did make their appearance they weren't disguised at all. They were dressed as common ordinary puddin'-thieves, save that the Possum carried a bran bag in his hand and the Wombat waved a white flag.

'Well, if this isn't too bad,' shouted Bill, enraged. 'What d'you mean, comin' along in this unexpected way without bein' disguised?'

'No, no,' sang out the Possum. 'No disguises to-day.'

'No fighting, either,' said the Wombat.

'No disguises, no fighting, and no puddin'-stealing,' said the Possum. 'Nothing but the fairest and most honourable dealings.'

'If you ain't after our Puddin', then what are you after?' demanded Bill.

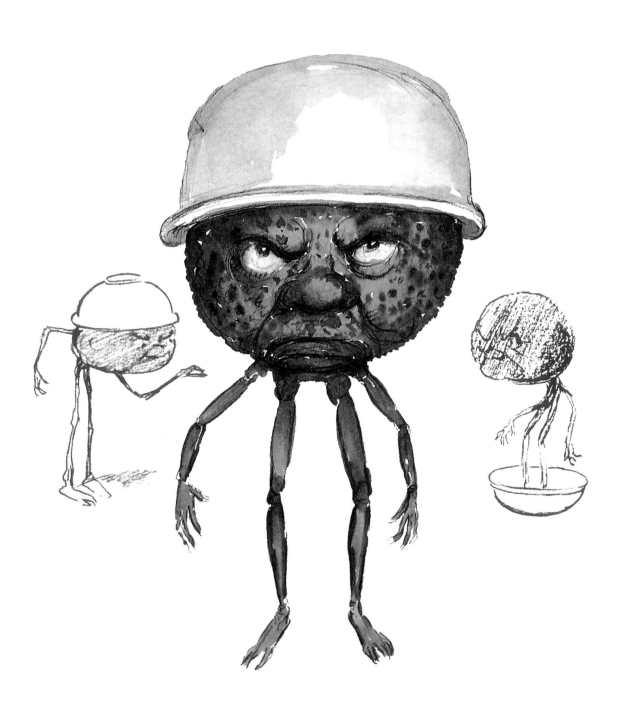

'We're after bringing you a present in this bag,' said the Possum.

'Absurd,' said Bill. 'Puddin'-thieves don't give presents away.'

'Don't say that, Bill,' said the Possum, solemnly. 'If you only knew what noble intentions we have, you'd be ashamed of them words.'

'You'd blush to hear your voice a-utterin' of them,' said the Wombat.

'I can't make this out at all,' said Bill, scratching his head. 'The idea of a puddin'-thief offering a man a present dumbfounds me, as the saying goes.'

'No harm is intended,' said the Possum, and the Wombat added: 'Harm is as far from our thoughts as from the thoughts of angels.'

'Well, well,' said Bill, at length. 'I'll just glance at it first, to see what it's like.'

But the Possum shook his head. 'No, no, Bill,' he said, 'no glancing,' and the Wombat added: 'To prove that no deception is intended, all heads must look in the bag together.'

'What's to be done about this astoundin' predicament?' said Bill. 'If there is a present, of course we may as well have it. If there ain't a present, of course we shall simply have to punch their snouts as usual.'

'One must confess,' said Bunyip Bluegum, 'to the prompting of a certain curiosity as to the nature of this present;' and Sam added, 'Anyway, there's no harm in having a look at it.'

'No harm whatever,' said the Possum, and he held the bag open invitingly. The Puddin'-owners hesitated a moment, but the

temptation was too strong, and they all looked in together. It was a fatal act. The Possum whipped the bag over their heads, the Wombat whipped a rope round the bag, and there they were, helpless.

The worst of it was that the Puddin', being too short to look in, was left outside, and the puddin'-thieves grabbed him at once and ran off like winking. To add to the Puddin'-owners' discomfiture there was a considerable amount of bran in the bag; and, as Bill said afterwards, if there's anything worse than losing a valuable Puddin', it's bran in the whiskers. They bounded and plunged about, but soon had to stop that on account of treading on each other's toes – especially Sam's, who endured agonies, having no boots on.

'What a frightful calamity,' groaned Bill, giving way to despair.

'It's worse than being chased by natives on the Limpopo River,' said Sam.

'It's worse than fighting Arabs single-handed,' croaked Bill.

'It's almost as bad as being pecked on the head by eagles,' said Sam, and in despair they sang in muffled tones –

'O what a fearful fate it is,　　'Our noble confidence has sent
　　O what a frightful fag,　　　　　Us on this fearful jag;
To have to walk about like this　In noble confidence we bent
　　All tied up in a bag.　　　　　　To look inside this bag.

'Deprived of air, in dark despair
　　Upon our way we drag;
Condemned for evermore to wear
　　This frightful, fearsome bag.'

Bunyip Bluegum reproved this faint-heartedness, saying, 'As our misfortunes are due to exhibiting too great a trust in scoundrels, so let us bear them with the greater fortitude. As in innocence we fell, so let our conduct in this hour of dire extremity be guided by the courageous endurance of men whose consciences are free from guilt.'

These fine words greatly stimulated the others, and they endured with fortitude walking on Sam's feet for an hour-and-a-half, when the sound of footsteps apprised them that a traveller was approaching.

This traveller was a grave, elderly dog named Benjimen Brandysnap, who was going to market with eggs. Seeing three people walking in a bag he naturally supposed they were practising for the sports, but on hearing their appeals for help he very kindly undid the rope.

'Preserver,' exclaimed Bill, grasping him by the hand.

'Noble being,' said Sam.

'Guardian angel of oppressed Puddin'-owners,' said Bunyip Bluegum.

Benjimen was quite overcome by these expressions of esteem, and handed round eggs, which were eaten on the spot.

'And now,' said Bill, again shaking hands with their preserver, 'I am about to ask you a most important question. Have you seen any puddin'-thieves about this mornin'?'

'Puddin'-thieves,' said Benjimen. 'Let me see. Now that you mention it, I remember seeing two puddin'-thieves at nine-thirty this morning. But they weren't stealing puddin's. They were engaged stealing a bag out of my stable. I was busy at the time whistling to the carrots, or I'd have stopped them.'

'This is most important information,' said Bill. 'It proves this must be the very bag they stole. In what direction did the scoundrels go, friend, after stealing your bag?'

'As I was engaged at the moment feeding the parsnips, I didn't happen to notice,' said Benjimen. 'But at this season puddin'-thieves generally go south-east, owing to the price of onions.'

'In that case,' said Bill, 'we shall take a course north-west, for it's my belief that havin' stolen our Puddin' they'll make back to winter quarters.'

'In order to exacerbate our just anger,' said Bunyip Bluegum 'let us sing as we go –

THE PUDDIN'-OWNERS' QUEST

'On a terrible quest we run north-west,
In a terrible rage we run;
With never a rest we run north-west
Till our terrible work is done.
Without delay
Away, away,
In a terrible rage we run all day.

'By our terrible zest you've doubtless guessed
That vengeance is our work;
For we seek the nest with terrible zest
Where the puddin'-snatchers lurk.
With rage, with gloom,
With fret and fume,
We seek the puddin'-snatchers' doom.'

They ran north-west for two hours without seeing a sign of the Puddin'-thieves. Benjimen ran with them to exact revenge for the theft of his bag. It was hot work running, and having no Puddin' they couldn't have lunch, but Benjimen very generously handed eggs all round again.

'Eggs is all very well,' said Bill, eating them in despair, 'but they don't come up to Puddin' as a regular diet, and all I can say is, that if that Puddin' ain't restored soon I shall go mad with grief.' 'I shall go mad with rage,' said Sam, and they both sang loudly –

'Go mad with grief or mad with rage,
It doesn't matter whether;
Our Puddin's left this earthly stage,
So in despair we must engage
To both go mad together.'

'I have a suggestion to make,' said Bunyip Bluegum, 'which will at once restore your wonted good-humour. Observe me.'

He looked about till he found a piece of board, and wrote this notice on it with his fountain pen —

A GRAND PROCESSION OF
THE AMALGAMATED SOCIETY OF
PUDDINGS WILL PASS HERE
AT 2.30 TO-DAY.

This he hung on a tree. 'Now,' said he, 'all that remains to be done is to hide behind this bush. The news of the procession will spread like wildfire through the district, and the puddin'-thieves, unable to resist such a spectacle, will come hurrying to view the procession. The rest will be simply a matter of springing out on them like lions.'

'Superbly reasoned,' said Bill, grasping Bunyip by the hand.

They all hid behind the bush, and a Crow, who happened to be passing, read the sign and flew off at once to spread the news through the district.

In fifteen minutes, by Bill's watch, the puddin'-thieves came running down the road, and took up a position on a stump to watch the procession. They had evidently been disturbed in the

very act of eating Puddin', for the Possum was still masticating a mouthful; and the Wombat had stuck the Puddin' in his hat, and put his hat on his head, which clearly proved him to be a very ill-bred fellow, for in good society wearing puddin's on the head is hardly ever done.

Bill and Sam, who were like bloodhounds straining in the leash, sprang out and confronted the scoundrels, while Bunyip and Ben got behind in order to cut off their retreat.

'We've got you at last,' said Bill, sparring up at the Possum with the fiercest activity. 'Out with our Puddin', or prepare for a punch on the snout.'

The Possum turned pale and the Wombat hastily got behind him.

'Puddin',' said the Possum, acting amazement, 'what strange request is this?'

'What means this strange request?' asked the Wombat.

'No bungfoodlin',' said Bill, sternly. 'Produce the Puddin' or prepare for death.'

'Before bringing accusations,' said the Possum, 'prove where the Puddin' is.'

'It's under that feller's hat,' roared Bill, pointing at the Wombat.

'Prove it,' said the Wombat.

'You can't wear hats that high, without there's Puddin's under them,' said Bill.

'That's not Puddin's,' said the Possum; 'that's ventilation. He wears his hat like that to keep his brain cool.'

'Very well,' said Bill. 'I call on Ben Brandysnap, as an independent witness whose bag has been stolen, to prove what's under that hat.'

Ben put on his spectacles in order to study the Wombat carefully, and gravely pronounced this judgment –

'When you see a hat
Stuck up like that
You remark with some surprise,
"Has he been to a shop,
And bought for his top
A hat of the largest size?"

'Or else you say,
As you note the way
He wears it like a wreath,
"It cannot be fat
That bulges his hat;
He's got something underneath."

'But whether or not

It's a Puddin' he's got

Can only be settled by lifting his pot.

Or by taking a stick,

A stone or a brick,

And hitting him hard on the head with it quick.

If he yells, you hit fat,

If he doesn't, well that

Will prove it's a Puddin' that's under his hat.'

'Now are you satisfied?' asked Bill, and they all shouted –

'Hurrah! hurray!

Just listen to that;

He knows the way

To bell the cat.

You'd better obey

His judgment pat,

'Without delay

Remove the hat;

It's tit-for-tat

We tell you flat,

You'll find it pay

To lift your hat.

'Obey the mandate of our chosen lawyer,

Remove that hat, or else we'll do it faw yer.'

Morris Gleitzman

BLABBER MOUTH

ILLUSTRATIONS BY BETINA OGDEN

Rowena dreads what her eccentric, apple-farming dad will do when he comes to the sports carnival at her new school.

I T was fine.

Mostly.

Sort of.

At least Dad didn't sing.

And when he put his hand down the front of Mrs Cosgrove's dress, he was just trying to be helpful.

I'd better start at the beginning.

I got up really early and ironed Dad a shirt. One without tassels. Or pictures of cowgirls riding horses at rodeos. It had metal corners on the collar, but I hoped people would think Dad was just careful about his shirts fraying.

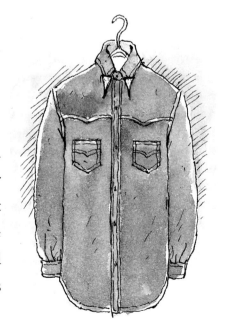

While he was getting dressed, Dad announced he was going to wear a special belt buckle to bring me luck in the race. I was worried for a moment, but when he came into the kitchen he was wearing one I hadn't seen before – a kangaroo in mid-hop.

I gave him a hug, partly because it was a kind thought, and partly because I was relieved he wasn't wearing the grinning skeleton riding the Harley Davidson.

In the truck on the way into town he played me one of his Carla Tamworth tapes. It was the song about the marathon runner who realises at the end of the race he's left his sweetheart's photo in the motel room so he runs all the way back to get it.

I could see Dad was trying to inspire me.

I wished he'd stop.

'Dad,' I said, 'I'm only in the hundred metres. And I'm up against an ace runner.'

Dad grinned and played the song again.

'What it's saying, Tonto,' he said, 'is that we can do all kinds of stuff even when we think we can't.'

If it was saying that, I thought, it'd be about a girl at a sports carnival who manages to persuade her dad not to upset the other spectators.

When we got to the school oval, the first event was just about to start. Kids and parents were standing around talking quietly, teachers were hurrying about with stopwatches and clipboards, and Ms Dunning was telling Darryn Peck off for throwing a javelin in the boys' toilet.

'Well, Tonto,' asked Dad, 'are we going to stand here all day

like stunned fungi or are you going to introduce me to some of your classmates?'

I tried to explain that it wasn't a good time as the sack race was about to start and everyone was very tense.

'You're the only one who looks tense, Tonto,' said Dad. 'You can't win a race with your guts in a knot. Come on, lie down and we'll do some breathing exercises.'

Dad took his hat off, stretched out on the ground on his back, and started taking deep breaths through his nose.

I saw other parents glancing over with puzzled expressions, and other kids smirking.

'Dad,' I said, 'if you don't get up I'm going to drop a heavy metal ball on your head.'

Dad shrugged and got up.

As he did, Ms Dunning came over to us.

'G'day Ro,' she said. 'G'day Mr Batts.'

I explained to Dad who she was.

'G'day,' said Dad. 'Kenny Batts.' He grinned and shook her hand for about two months. 'Ro's told me what a top teacher you are.'

Ms Dunning grinned modestly and Dad turned to me and winked and asked me if Ms Dunning was married.

For the millionth time in my life I was grateful that Dad talks to me with his hands.

But I still wanted to go and bury myself in the long-jump pit.

'I can see I'm going to have to learn some sign language,' grinned Ms Dunning. Then she excused herself and hurried away because she'd just seen Darryn Peck holding a starting pistol to another kid's head.

'Nice teacher,' said Dad. 'OK, let's mingle.'

As usual I was torn between going off and sitting in the toilets so no one could see I was with him, and sticking with him to try and keep him out of trouble.

As usual I stuck with him.

He walked over to some parents talking to their kid.

He'd already said 'G'day, nice day for it,' and stuck out his hand when I realised the kid was Amanda Cosgrove, the hundred metres champion.

And Mr Cosgrove had already shaken Dad's hand and was already looking Dad up and down with a sour expression on his face when I recognised his brown suit and realised he was the bloke who'd glared at us as we were being chucked out of the milk bar.

I smiled nervously at Amanda, but she was staring at the ground. Either that or Dad's goanna-skin boots.

'G'day,' said Dad, shaking Mrs Cosgrove's hand.

Mrs Cosgrove was looking very nervous and gripping her handbag very tightly.

'Nice suit,' said Dad, feeling Mr Cosgrove's lapel and winking at him. 'Bet it cost a few bob. Criminal, the price of clothes these days.'

'I own a menswear store,' replied Mr Cosgrove coldly.

'You'd be right then, eh?' said Dad, giving him a friendly nudge. 'Listen, you might be able to help me out. Last year at a Carla Tamworth concert one of the backup singers was wearing this unreal pink satin shirt with black fringing on the back and a black guitar on the front. I've been looking everywhere for one. You wouldn't have one in stock, would you?'

'We don't stock satin shirts,' said Mr Cosgrove, even more coldly.

Dad stared at him, amazed. 'You should,' he said, 'they're big sellers. I buy one every couple of months.'

Mr Cosgrove didn't look as though he was going to rush out and order a truckload.

Amanda nudged me gently. 'It's our race,' she said softly.

She was right.

Mr Fowler was calling through his megaphone for all the contestants in the hundred metre races. Kids were lining up in their different age groups near the starting line.

I was just about to go with Amanda to join them when I saw Dad staring at Mrs Cosgrove's chest.

Crawling across her dress was a small greyish-brown moth.

Dad took a step closer to her.

'Don't move,' he said.

Mrs Cosgrove froze with fear.

'Codling moth,' explained Dad. 'If you've got any apple or pear trees at home these buggers'll go through 'em like guided missiles.'

'We haven't,' said Mr Cosgrove.

'I have,' said Dad, and made a grab for the moth.

Before he could get his hand to it, the moth fluttered in through the armhole of Mrs Cosgrove's dress.

Mrs Cosgrove gave a little scream.

'Hold still,' said Dad, 'I'll get it.'

He grabbed Mrs Cosgrove's shoulder and stuck his hand into the armhole.

Mrs Cosgrove gave a louder scream.

Mr Cosgrove grabbed Dad and pulled him away. 'You be careful, mister,' he snapped.

'It's OK,' said Dad, 'I've got it.'

He showed Mr Cosgrove the squashed moth between his fingers.

'You,' Mr Cosgrove said loudly, glaring at Dad, 'are a rude, unpleasant, badly dressed hoon. Why don't you back off, go home, and leave us in peace?'

Dad stared at Mr Cosgrove, bewildered, and he looked so hurt I felt like crying.

'Amanda Cosgrove and Rowena Batts to the starting line,' boomed Mr Fowler's voice through the megaphone.

Then Dad stopped looking hurt.

He glared at Mr Cosgrove. 'Pull your head in,' he said, 'I was only trying to help.'

He turned to me. 'The bloke's a cheesebrain,' he said with his hands. 'Don't let him spoil your race. Get out there and show 'em your dust, Tonto.'

He glared at Mr Cosgrove again and walked off.

I followed Amanda to the starting line and glanced at her but she didn't look at me.

I stood there while Darryn Peck won his race and crowed about it for several minutes.

I hardly noticed.

I was seeing something else in my head.

Me doing what I should have done ages ago.

Telling Dad to back off and stop scaring people away.

Making him listen.

And him doing what I've always feared he'd do.

Looking hurt like he did with Mr Cosgrove but ten times worse because it was me, then glaring at me and walking away.

The gun went off and I leapt forward and squashed the picture in my head.

Suddenly I felt so angry I wanted to scream, but of course I couldn't so I concentrated on pounding my legs into the ground as hard as I could.

The kids on either side dropped back and suddenly the only one I could see out of the corner of my eye was Amanda Cosgrove, and then she disappeared too.

I was in front.

Then I saw Dad, up ahead by the finish line, a big grin on his face, eyes gleaming with excitement, jumping up and down and waving his arms at me.

And another picture flashed into my head.

Dad, after I'd won, sharing his excitement with the other parents.

Slapping them on the back so they spilt their drinks.

Digging them in the ribs so they dropped their sandwiches.

Sticking his hand into their armholes until they all ran for their cars and roared away as fast as they could and had serious accidents on the way home so all their kids had to go to special schools and I was the only one who didn't.

And suddenly I could hardly move my legs any more, and as I stumbled over the finish line Amanda Cosgrove was there at my side.

∽

Emily Rodda

PIGS MIGHT FLY

ILLUSTRATED BY NOELA YOUNG

'I wish something would happen,' said Rachel one rainy Saturday morning. And that was the beginning of her extraordinary adventure . . .

RACHEL blinked. Something had happened to the light. It had spread, and brightened. Everything looked pale green. She blinked again and looked slowly around. This wasn't right! Her room had disappeared. Her bed had disappeared. She was in the middle of a broad, green field, in her pyjamas, sitting astride a –

The unicorn turned its head and looked at her gravely. It snorted softly. Its golden horn glittered in the sunlight, its white mane stirred gently in the breeze.

'Oh, no!' whispered Rachel. 'What have I done?'

The great muscles in the unicorn's back twitched and it began to walk slowly forward, placing its feet gently on the tussocky green grass.

Rachel had only ridden a horse once before – and that was a Shetland pony. Only half a horse compared with this huge

creature. She clutched desperately at the silky mane and hung on tightly with her knees. What else could she do? She couldn't possibly jump off. It was a long way to the ground.

The unicorn moved on quietly. And then Rachel heard the first, faint grunting. She knew where it was coming from, but at first she just couldn't bring herself to look. She screwed up her eyes and counted to ten. Then she opened one eye. Oh, no! She quickly shut it again. But it was no good. Seeing was believing, and she had to know the worst. She held on tightly to the unicorn's mane, counted to ten again, gritted her teeth, and looked up into the blue sky.

The pigs were there, sailing plumply, pinkly, just above her, grunting softly to themselves. As she watched, one rolled over in a somersault and kicked its trotters at the sun with a little squeak of pleasure.

The unicorn pricked its ears and began to trot. Rachel held on grimly, bouncing on the broad, slippery back. No point in calling out – she couldn't see a single living creature who might help her. The pigs were having far too good a time even to notice

she was there. She was in a strange field, in her pyjamas, riding on a unicorn!

'This must be a dream,' thought Rachel suddenly. 'Of course! That means I'll wake up soon, and there's nothing to worry about. It doesn't feel like a dream, but these things just don't happen in real life, so it must be.' This thought comforted her very much. She noticed her drink bottle sticking out of her pyjama pocket. Somehow that comforted her too. Something from home. What a shame it was empty. Her fright had made her thirsty.

The unicorn nickered warningly and quickened its pace. Rachel looked over its arching neck and saw that it had reached the crest of a hill and was heading for a small white house tucked away in the valley below. A pink blob bobbed around in the sky above the house. Another pig, for heaven's sake! And even as she watched she saw that the wind was bringing more of them into view, tumbling and rolling. Little pigs, squealing and squeaking in excitement, medium-sized pigs, their legs spread out blissfully to catch the cool breeze, a few very big, whiskery old pigs, sailing along in majestic fashion, looking neither to right nor left. One great pig, the grandfather of all pigs, stood massively on the hillside, watching them with wise little eyes.

The unicorn broke into a gallop. Its hooves pounded on the grass, and its mane flew. The drink bottle flew from Rachel's pocket and fell onto the ground. She clung desperately to the unicorn's neck, hunched over like a jockey. She felt that any moment she would fall.

'I suppose if I did fall I'd wake up!' she thought to herself. 'Maybe I should just let go.'

But somehow she couldn't bring herself to try out the experiment, and while she was still thinking about it and trying to persuade herself to be brave and take the risk, the unicorn slowed to a canter, then fell into a trot. They had almost reached the house.

The unicorn stopped and pawed at the ground. It nickered gently, and the muscles of its shoulders twitched. Rachel slid cautiously from its back, and jumped to the ground.

The white house stood before her, its green-painted door firmly closed. A light glowed at one of the front windows, but the whole place had the air of being closed up tight, as if the owners had no wish to be disturbed. Rachel walked down the neat brick path and nervously put her hand on the old black doorknocker. She looked nervously behind her. The unicorn was watching. It nodded its head and snorted softly through its nose in an encouraging way. Rachel turned back to the door, raised the knocker and tapped three times.

'I'll go!' called a woman's voice inside the house. Steps approached the door and it opened just a crack.

A plump old face framed with crinkly, wispy white hair peeped through the crack, and pale blue eyes gazed in vague surprise at Rachel.

'Excuse me . . .' Rachel began.

The door was flung wide. The old lady beamed and held out her arms.

'Gloria! You're here! Oh, I knew it! I said to Bertie, one piggy day, I said, you never know . . . Come in, dear, come in . . . Bertie! Bertie! Gloria's here!'

'But . . .' Rachel stammered.

'Come in, pet, come in! Don't stand out there in the pigs, for goodness' sake.' The old lady started ushering Rachel inside as if protecting her from a hurricane.

Rachel took one last, confused look at the green hills basking under the perfect sky and stepped into the house.

'Thanks!' the old lady called nervously to the unicorn. 'Thanks very much! We'll be right now. No need to wait. Thank you.'

The unicorn nodded in dignified fashion and began to walk quietly away.

'It's just as well to be polite, pet, isn't it?' the old lady said to Rachel in a lower voice. 'They're that moody.'

'Ah . . . I don't . . .' Rachel shook her head helplessly.

'What's going on? Enid? Have you got that door open? Are you bonkers, woman?' called someone irritably from the back of the house.

'Bertie!' exclaimed the old lady excitedly. 'Look here! It's Gloria, Gloria!'

Rachel tugged timidly at her sleeve.

'I'm sorry, but I'm not Gloria,' she whispered. 'My name's Rachel.'

The old lady turned surprised blue eyes towards her.

'Not . . . you're not Gloria? But . . .'

'Of course it's not Gloria, you silly old biddie! Don't hold the door open like that!' bawled an exasperated voice. A tall, thin old man stood, hands on hips, at the end of the hall. He beckoned impatiently to them.

'Come into the kitchen, and for goodness' sake, shut the door! Dear oh dear. Gloria!' He shook his head. 'Gloria'd be a grown woman by now, Mum, you know that!' he roared. 'Bring the girl in here!' He stomped off into the back of the house again.

'Oh dear . . . I'm a silly old duck. It's this weather,' said the old lady. 'Come into the kitchen, love, and tell us what we can do for you. Come on. I'm sorry. I got you mixed up with someone else. See, I've been hoping . . .' she shook her head. 'Anyhow, come out the back, and I'll get you a glass of milk. Eh?'

'Oh . . . um . . . it's all right,' said Rachel nervously, glancing at the front door. She was convinced that both of these people were crazy, or at least had a few screws loose in their think

saucepans, as Dad would have said. 'I'd better ... ' She started walking back to the door.

'You can't go out in that, pet! It's blowing up to a real grunter. The pigs are up, love. Didn't you see? UEF 7 or 8 by now, I bet. Your mum and dad must be that worried about you. We'd better ring them up. If we can get through,' Enid added doubtfully.

She bustled off down the dark hall and Rachel followed, feeling like Alice in Wonderland. She didn't understand any of this, and didn't like it at all.

A.B. Facey

A FORTUNATE LIFE

COLOUR ILLUSTRATION BY ANNE SPUDVILAS

BLACK AND WHITE ILLUSTRATIONS BY BETINA OGDEN

*As a cook's assistant on a cattle drive up the north-west of
Western Australia, Bert becomes lost in the desert.*

DAYLIGHT finally came. There were no cattle and I couldn't see any tracks; it was still raining and there was running water everywhere. I tied Dinnertime to a bush and climbed up to the top of a high ironstone hill. All I could see from the top was mountainous country in all directions. I was lost. I was also cold, wet and hungry, and very frightened.

I scrambled down to my pony and climbed on her back. I had been told that if you get lost while on horseback, you should give the horse its head and it will take you home. This theory was no good with Dinnertime – she only took me where there was plenty of feed. I let her eat as much as she wanted and walked for a time to get the warmth back into my legs and body. Then I rode to the top of some other high hills, but still to no avail.

I kept Dinnie going and going until we came to a gorge with large granite boulders on each side. There were large caves under the boulders, big enough for a horse to walk into. Now it was getting late and I decided to camp there for the night. I unsaddled Dinnie, and tethered her near the cave. Thank goodness I had the tether rope, because without Dinnie all would be lost for me. But Dinnie pawed the ground and came inside the cave and lay down to rest. Some of my fear left me at this, and after a while I went to sleep.

When I woke it was daylight and still raining. The gorge had water running through it like a little river. The sun was completely hidden; I was unable to tell north from south, or east from west. After giving Dinnie a longer tether rope, so she could reach some grass, I sat thinking what to do. I thought, If the grass is good for Dinnie, it is good enough for me. I put some in my mouth and chewed it. The juice tasted nice but no matter how hard I tried, I couldn't swallow the grass. At least I had no water troubles. It would be terrible to be lost like this with no water.

When Dinnie stopped eating, I saddled her up and rode all the rest of that day towards what I thought was the west. I rode up on to high hills and peaks along valleys, but saw only kangaroos by the hundreds, a few emus and a few wild horses. Not a sign of a track.

The rain stopped just before dark. The wind stopped too and everything was still and quiet. All I could hear was a dingo howling and another answering in the distance. I came across a thick patch of scrub and decided to camp there for the night. I broke off a pile of scrub and made a place to lie down. I tethered Dinnie and spent my second night alone.

In the morning the sky was clear. I waited for the sun, looking to where I expected it to rise. I got the surprise of my life. It rose behind me. This confused me completely. I was absolutely lost. I wondered what I should do. Then I decided that if I kept travelling in one direction, I must come across some road or river that I could follow back, out of this hopeless situation I had got myself into.

I saddled Dinnie and rode off in what I thought was a south-west direction. Dinnie walked at a very lively pace along valleys and over high hills and flat scrubby country. Then she pricked up her ears and stopped still, as if she had spotted something. I got off her back and tied her to a clump of scrub, then I sneaked back to see what was there, being very careful not to be seen. Luckily the wind was blowing towards me so whatever it was wouldn't be able to smell me. For a few minutes I couldn't make out anything, then I saw something. I moved closer. It was a black man, very wild-looking, with a long bushy beard. I was scared stiff. I stopped where I was, watching, and after a few minutes he picked up the hindquarters of a large kangaroo and a bundle of spears and set off over a rise.

When I was sure he was gone I went to the spot where he had been and found the front half of a kangaroo he had just skinned. I noticed that he hadn't taken the liver, so, being starving, I took it out and ate it all. Then I took the rest of the carcass down to where I had left Dinnie, tied it to the saddle and walked, leading the pony.

All of a sudden I became very ill. I felt as if I had been poisoned. I lay down near a large granite boulder and vomited – I couldn't stop. I felt too weak to do anything. Finally, I managed to get up. It was now well into the afternoon. I untied the kangaroo from the saddle, took the saddle off and rested it against a boulder. Then I tethered Dinnie to where she could get plenty of good feed. Funny, I wasn't frightened – I just didn't care what became of me.

Finally I fell asleep, and woke just before daylight, on the fourth day, with terrible pains in my stomach. I felt very faint and it was nearly midday before the pains eased. Dinnie stood looking at me. She couldn't understand why I hadn't shifted her tether to fresh grass. Late in the afternoon I felt a little better, and getting some sharp-edged stones, I set about bruising pieces of the flesh of the kangaroo carcass to chew into small pieces later. By the time I had finished, the sun was close to setting. I saddled up and followed a small running stream hoping to find a better camping place. Just before dark I came to a beautiful valley with a watercourse almost big enough to be called a river. There was plenty of feed for Dinnie so I camped there. I unsaddled and tethered her and made myself a place to lie down for the night. I tried chewing some of the kangaroo meat, and I couldn't help

thinking that perhaps I had made a mistake in hiding from that black man. He may have been able to help me – and almost anything would be better than what I was going through now. Finally I dozed off to sleep.

When daylight came I shifted Dinnie's tether rope and had a drink of water out of the stream. I was in the fifth day now and there was no sign of anything that would help me – no tracks, no cattle, no way of knowing how far I had travelled or in what direction. I made up my mind that no matter what happened, I would not leave the watercourse, but keep following the direction of the flowing water. It must eventually take me somewhere.

I saddled Dinnie and set off again. I kept on chewing the small pieces of meat, and whenever I stopped to rest or have a drink, I would chew grass or the leaves of the scrub bushes, since my stomach had settled down. It was terribly hot so I had to rest every two or three hours, and the flies and mosquitoes were very bad.

The going was very rough – hills with huge boulders all over them – then a valley would open out into a large, scrubby plain with the everwinding watercourse travelling on and on.

The next day was very similar to the fifth. The sun was so hot that I was forced to lie up for about five hours in the middle of the day. That night I found a sand patch close to the bank of the watercourse that was nice and soft to lie on. It was a long time before I went to sleep. My kangaroo meat supplies were very low and all sorts of frightening thoughts came to me. A person would have to be lost like I was to really know what it was like – it was dreadful.

When I awakened on the seventh day I got a shock. Dinnie was over the other side of the stream. I thought she must have got off the tether. Then two black men jumped me, one from each side. These black men looked very wild. They wore only loincloths out of kangaroo skins, and they all had beards. I yelled, 'Let me go!' and tried to struggle free, but they held me and one of them called out to a third man who was on the other side of the stream with Dinnie. I didn't understand their language. The one with Dinnie brought her back over the stream, then they put the saddle on her and one of the men made signs to me. I realized that they wanted me to get on Dinnie's back. I did this, then one of them took the reins and led her. We left the watercourse and travelled north.

I had been scared many times in my short life, but nothing like I was now. They ran on bare feet, and Dinnie had to trot to keep up with them most of the time. They travelled towards a large hill. It took us about two hours to get to the top. There I

dismounted and one of the black men unsaddled Dinnie. Then one of them squatted and did something with a pile of dry sticks and scrub so that, after a few minutes, smoke started rising. They gathered some green scrub and bushes and heaped them in the fire, which made a thick white smoke. Then one of them took the saddle cloth from Dinnie and kept putting it on and off the fire. It was at this moment that I realized, with relief, that they had built the fire to make smoke signals.

Suddenly one of them gave a shout and patted me on the shoulder and pointed at something in the distance. Then I saw it.

Little clouds were going up into the air at small intervals from a hill top to the north-west, some three or four miles away.

One of the black men put the saddle on Dinnie and the other two put the fire out by throwing earth on it. We set off towards where the other smoke signals had been. It was amazing how they could travel over prickly scrub and stony ground with their bare feet. We stopped every two or three hours for the men to rest. Every time they stopped they would let Dinnie feed. The blacks had no food, and how they kept going I'll never know. After dark they slowed to a walk. Then, while travelling on a rise, one of them pointed to a small light in the distance. He squeezed my leg. The gesture conveyed to me that we were close to the end of our journey. The fear had left me now; I knew the blacks were my friends.

An hour or so later we arrived at a large blacks' camp. There were several large fires burning and about thirty dogs came towards us, barking. We were surrounded by dozens of blacks and then, to my surprise, out walked Stan Smith. 'Bert, you come with me,' he said. He took me to a fairly large mia-mia. Inside there were several older natives and they were all very pleased to see me. A middle-aged native woman came in with a bowl with some kind of dark fluid in it. She handed it to me. I looked at Stan and he said to drink it, it would do me good. I didn't like the look of it but it tasted fine.

After I had finished it, he said to me, 'You better not have any more, Bert. You'll have to be careful and start with only a little at a time for now.' I lay down on some skins with a rug spread over me. I was dog-tired and was soon sound asleep.

When I awoke next morning the sun was high in the sky. Stan came into the mia-mia and asked me how I felt. I told him I was still very tired but felt much better. While we were talking the native woman came back. This time she gave me some kangaroo steak and some kind of damper which tasted beautiful. Stan could talk the blacks' language and I asked him to thank the woman and the three men that found me.

You would have thought I was a king or something, the fuss they made. The chief, a large man, took me by the hand and wished me well, and made it clear that he and his people were my friends. The three men that had found me came and shook me by the hand and patted me on the shoulders in such a friendly, jolly manner. A few minutes later they fetched our horses and Stan said we must get back to the herd. After shaking hands with dozens of the blacks – men, women and children – we rode away.

The day was very hot and Stan said that the extra heat this time of the year was unusual – it could mean another storm. I said, 'I hope not. I've had enough storms to do me the rest of my life.' Then Stan asked me how I had managed to live. I told him how I had taken pieces off the kangaroo carcass and kept chewing them. He said, 'If you had approached the black he would have saved you then. All the blacks were on the lookout for you. They're all friendly. Don't take any notice of the tales that you hear.'

When I told Stan about deciding to follow the watercourse no matter what, he said that was good judgement and most likely saved my life. Stan was a good bushman and knew the country in the North like the back of his hand. He said, 'That watercourse

you followed was a branch of the Gascoyne River – the Lyons. Our herd should be travelling close to the other end of the Lyons about now.'

We camped for the night at a boundary rider's shack. Stan awakened me just after daylight; he estimated that we should catch the herd some time that day. Late in the afternoon we came across tracks made by the herd. Stan said that the tracks were a day old so we should catch up to them before dark. About sundown we reached the camp, close to the bend of a river. Stan told me again that this was the river I had been following. 'So,' he said, 'you were on your way to safety.'

∾

Graeme Base

THE SIGN OF
THE SEAHORSE

ILLUSTRATED BY THE AUTHOR

Our heroine, Pearl, falls in love with Corporal Bert, and the evil Groper
pays an unwelcome visit to the Seahorse Café.

THE Seahorse Café was the place where fine young fish would meet.
To spend the evening dancing to the latest Reeftown beat.
The rock was hard, the drinks were soft, the chairs were in between;
In short, the Seahorse was the place in which one should be seen.

The café sat upon a knoll, above the ebb and flow,
Unblemished by the poison that was taking hold below.
The band was hot, the place was cool, the atmosphere just right,
And all the fish would bop 'n' hop and boogie through the night.

The owner of the café was a fine, upstanding Trout,
Who had a lovely daughter and a son who seemed a lout.
She waitressed at the café and was cheerful, quick and bright;
But he had joined a Catfish Gang and stayed out late at night.

Despite the shock of spiky hair and earrings in his snout,
Young Finneus was really just your normal teenage Trout.
The Catfish Gang looked tough and mean – no manners, no respect.
But deep inside they meant no harm and dressed up for effect.

The daughter (we shall call her Pearl) would often stop and flirt,
With all the local Soldiercrabs, until she noticed Bert.
He looked the part: a clipped moustache, two eyes, eight boots, one glove.
And Pearl, who couldn't help herself, fell hopelessly in love.

That fateful night when Pearl and Bert first fell for one another,
And she gazed deep into his eyes, first one stalk then the other,
There came a crash, somebody screamed, and in the doorway stood,
The Groper and his henchfish – it was clear they meant no good.

The Groper was an ugly fish, with wicked, piggy eyes,
Possessed of bloated appetites, as witnessed by his size.
His pin-stripe suit was tailor-made, complete with matching tie:
Exactly what the well-dressed crook was wearing that July.

A savage-looking Swordfish stood a little to his right,
The kind of thug you wouldn't want to come across at night.
His sidekicks were a pair of Sharks, with dubious IQs,
Who dressed in stovepipe trousers and wore pointy, two-tone shoes.

The Groper owned the place next door, a sleezy, run-down bar,
Where low-life Slugs and Wentletraps made bootleg caviar.
He'd bought a lot of property in last October's crash,
And ran the sort of businesses where clients paid in cash.

The Groper said, 'You punks take heed! This warning is for you.
Stay outa this here café or your swimmin' days are through.
I own the only bar in town that's gonna jump and jive.
You come back here again and you ain't gonna stay alive!'

His bodyguards slicked back their hair and circled round the crowd,
As if to dare the customers to voice their thoughts aloud.
Then, roughing up a Seasnail who was less than half their height,
The Sharks rejoined their master and stepped out into the night.

∽

Tim Winton

THE BUGALUGS
BUM THIEF

ILLUSTRATED BY CAROL PELHAM-THORMAN

Skeeta Anderson wakes up one summer morning to find that part of him is gone, something he thought he'd never miss — his bum.

S KEETA lived in a small town by the sea. The town was called Bugalugs. No one could remember who was to blame for thinking up such a dumb name for a town, and even if they *could* remember, no one was going to own up to it. Because the people of Bugalugs were a bit proud. They were nice folks, but just a teeny bit vain.

Bugalugs was three streets wide and was built next to a beautiful bay where fishing boats anchored. Behind the town was a great desert of white dunes.

Every morning, before the sun came up over the dunes, the fishermen of Bugalugs went out to catch crayfish. They put fresh bait in their traps every day and the little red critters made gutses of themselves. As all sensible people know, a cray will eat anything except football boots, so bait is not hard to find. Every day crayfish were pulled from the traps, still munching, and were sent all over the world so people could munch on *them*. That's how it was every day at Bugalugs.

Except today.

Skeeta went to the window and saw Billy Marbles trying to ride past on his bike. Billy was sliding all over the place, with his knees hanging over the handlebars, and there was Billy's sister Mavis walking to school with a big dent in the back of her dress.

Skeeta ran out into the street, holding up his PJ's, and right away he saw it. The whole town was the same. No bums!

He ran inside and got dressed quickly. With some string he tied his trousers on.

Then he ran to his best mate's house.

Mick Misery, his best mate, was always getting a hiding. Mick's mum was a real smacker. Smacking was her hobby. She walloped Mick for being early, she whacked him for being late. But this morning she wasn't getting anywhere at all. When Skeeta arrived, Mick's mum was swinging away but every hit just swished past because Mick Misery was *bumless*.

Mrs Misery gave up glumly and sent them off to school. Mick whistled like a drunk canary but Skeeta was worried.

Maybe it's the ozone layer, he thought. Or perhaps we're under attack from aliens. But there had to be an easier answer.

It was an awful day at school. With nothing to sit on or hold their pants up with, the kids at Bugalugs Primary didn't get time to learn much. At lunch, Billy Marbles couldn't play doogs at all. As any sensible person knows, a bum gives you balance and you can't be school marble champ without balance. The footy team was useless, the netballers got depressed.

During spelling, Mr Wally's shorts suddenly sprang off their safety pins and went scurrying down his long hairy legs like rats out of a tree. The kids laughed. They cacked themselves. *And* they all went home with piles of homework so big they needed their dads' wheelbarrows to get it all home.

After school, instead of doing his homework, Skeeta Anderson decided to do some detective work. He wrote it all out on a piece

of paper. No one was talking about it all, embarrassed as they were, but it was pretty clear to Skeeta that:

1. at least 169 bums are missing
2. scientific instruments show no alien interference
3. binoculars show no missing bots plugging up the hole in the ozone layer

So, he figured: someone must have them. Someone must have burgled them, sneaked into everyone's bedroom with a torch and a pair of salad tongs and got away with the lot!

But Skeeta was a clever kid, a bit of a scientist, really. Because, as any sensible person knows, you can't hide a townful of bums very easily. And in a town where barely anyone has a pair of buttocks to their name, a person getting about still wearing one was definitely SUSPICIOUS.

So Skeeta wired on a pair of running shorts and began to investigate.

Ruth Park

THE MUDDLE-HEADED WOMBAT

ILLUSTRATED BY NOELA YOUNG

At the police station, where they were taken because they'd been busking, Mouse and Wombat meet a miserable grey tabby cat.

MOUSE tweaked at the Sergeant's shoe-laces.

'If no one else wants that cat,' it said, 'may I have him?' The Sergeant was pleased. He did not really want a police station cat because he had one already. But Wombat felt very jealous and bristly. He made a grumble-umble sound deep in his middle.

'Why do you want a cat when you've got me, Mouse, eh?' he asked.

'Because he's such a skinny, squeaky, plain little cat,' explained Mouse. 'Poor thing.'

Wombat made the grumble-umble noise again, and this time it got mixed up with the mouth organ and with one last horrid drone the mouth organ became silent.

'See what you've made me do?' scolded Wombat. 'Now I can't play on my breath, and how will we get pennies to buy a bike with red wheels?'

But Mouse wasn't listening. It had scampered over to the cat and was bouncing up and down and twinkling its spectacles.

'Would you like to come and live with Wombat and me and be our second-best friend and have adventures, and save up for a bike with red wheels?'

The cat nodded.

'What's your name?' asked Mouse.

'Vernon la Puss,' said the cat in a low trembling voice.

'Oh, it is not,' said Wombat, 'you're making up stories. I can tell by your droopy whiskers. Haven't you a sensibubble name like Mouse or Wombat?'

The cat wiped away a tear. 'I just made it up because it sounds

so grand. My name's really just Tabby Cat, and nobody loves me.'

'Come on, then,' said Mouse, 'and Wombat and I will love you.'

Wombat wasn't a bit sure that he wanted to love Tabby Cat. He knew he didn't want his nice little Mouse to love Tabby Cat. He felt very jealous. He wasn't even very pleased when the kind police sergeant gave him a water-pistol he'd found a long time before. He trundled along the road behind Tabby Cat and Mouse, and grumble-umbled to himself.

Mouse knew stray cats are usually hungry. Mouse bought some fish for Tabby, who had brightened up a lot since he had found some friends. Mouse also bought some orange drink for Wombat.

'Now, let's be happy!'

'I'm happy,' said Tabby. 'Fish is my favourite fruit!'

Suddenly Wombat felt so jealous he couldn't bear it any more. He dipped the water-pistol into his orange juice, filled it up, and shot Tabby in the waistcoat.

It was quite the most terrible thing he had ever done. Mouse didn't squeak to him for hours. As for Tabby, he licked and picked and picked and licked and still he felt sticky and orange-y.

Wombat was ashamed of himself.

'I'm very sorry, Tabby,' he said. 'Would you like me to wash you with soap and water and peg you out by the ears to dry?'

Tabby gave a miaow of terror. He darted up a tree and sat there crying.

'Nobody loves me. I told you. People *always* shoo me away and stand on my tail and shoot me with orange drink. Oh, I wish I weren't me!'

The Mouse tapped its pink foot in a fierce way. 'I'm ashamed of you, Wombat. Now, what can we do to help Tabby?'

Then it had an idea.

'What about a vacuum cleaner?'

'What's a what'sname, Mouse, eh?' asked Wombat hopefully.

'It's a sort of machine that sucks the dust out of carpets. If we used one on Tabby Cat, we could get every scrap of orange off his fur.'

'Let's try it on Wombat first,' said Tabby. 'I'm a delicate pussy.'

Wombat didn't mind. Wombat very much wanted to help. They went to a shop that sold carpets and explained to the man what they wanted to do. He was very helpful. He turned on the carpet cleaner and Tabby began to run the nozzle up and down Wombat's thick, tously, brown hair. It tickled Wombat very much. He rolled on the floor giggling. Mouse was delighted.

'You look so handsome, Wombat! Oh, I wish I weren't a small animal! Then I could be vacuumed, too.'

Then it was Tabby's turn.

'You be careful, Wombat. I don't want my ears turned inside-out or my whiskers knotted.'

Wombat turned on the cleaner. He went up and down, up and down Tabby's back.

'There are lots of grey spots here and I want to get them off.'

'You silly old muddle-head,' cried Tabby, 'those spots grow on me! After all, I *am* a tabby cat.'

'Don't you tell me I've got a head like a muddle,' growled Wombat. '*You've* got a head like a bicycle seat.'

Just then the nozzle fell off the vacuum cleaner, and poor Tabby flew straight up the pipe.

There was a gurgly sound in the pipe, and then the cleaner went on buzzing as though nothing had happened. Wombat turned the cleaner off, and he and Mouse peered down the pipe.

'Oh, Wombat, you are awful!' said Mouse, but it couldn't help giggling.

'Is it nice in there, Tabby?' called Wombat. 'I wish I could get in there and listen to the motor humming.'

But Tabby didn't answer. Mouse and Wombat sat down and looked at the cleaner for a while, then they thought that perhaps they'd better unscrew it and see how Tabby was getting along. Luckily the first thing Wombat unscrewed was the bit at the end where you take out the dust. Out came all kinds of interesting things; little balls of cotton, scraps of straw, pins and tacks, and a great, furry, grey wad of dust.

'Oooh, Tabby,' whispered Mouse, 'that isn't *you?*'

The furry ball of dust gave a great sneeze.

'We found him,' beamed Wombat, 'aren't we terribubbly smart?'

Some of the dust fell off and there was Tabby, wearing a woolly grey overcoat of dust, and a little beret of fluff on his head. Two yellow eyes glared out of the dust. Wombat was very surprised.

'However did you get so dirty, Tabby? I thought the middle of a cleaner would be as clean as clean.'

Tabby sneezed. 'I shall never forgive you, Wombat!' he said.

'But Tabby, I didn't put you inside the cleaner. I just pointed it at you and in you flew, like a bird, Tab.'

Tabby twitched his ears and out fluttered some pieces of red

and blue wool that had come out of the carpet.

'I'm not going to be friends with you, Wombat. Not if you go down on bended paws.'

Wombat took off his hat and began to cry into it.

'Perhaps I *have* a head like a muddle. I *am* sorry, Tabby. Don't be cross, Tabby.'

'He didn't mean to be unkind,' pleaded Mouse.

Tabby twitched his whiskers haughtily. The dust flew out in clouds.

'A cat has his pride,' he said. 'Good-bye forever.'

Mouse was small, but it was smart. It knew Tabby really didn't want to go away. So it said sadly:

'What a pity! I thought you could have your photograph taken when we have ours done. I *would* like a photograph of you, Tabby dear.'

Wombat stopped crying. He was about to say, 'What photograph?' but Mouse bit him on the toe just in time to stop him. Mouse had a feeling that Tabby Cat was very conceited, so it said even more sadly:

'Well, good-bye, Tabby dear. Don't let us stop you.'

'We-ell,' said Tabby, 'I wouldn't mind having a picture of myself to send to my Uncle Tom.'

Wombat was delighted. 'You lucky, lucky puss to have a nuncle, I haven't anyone. Is he a cat like you?'

'Silly,' said Tabby. He curled up his whiskers. 'I just *might* get my picture taken, Mouse, to please you.'

Mouse knew they had just enough money to pay a photographer. The bike with red wheels would have to wait.

The photographer was pleased to see them. He arranged Tabby looking at a flower.

'Just pretend it's a sardine,' said Wombat, 'and you'll look lovely.'

Tabby showed all his sharp teeth in a very sweet smile, the camera clicked, and it was all over.

'Oh, how happy Uncle Tom will be when he gets a picture of handsome me!' said Tabby as he jumped down from the chair. Now it was Mouse's turn. Mouse arranged its ears and its whiskers, draped its tail gracefully over one arm, smiled when it was told, and was photographed.

'What a very intelligent small animal!' said the photographer.

Now it was Wombat's turn. He would not take off his old straw hat.

'But you must,' said Tabby. 'Otherwise you'll look just like a haystack.'

Wombat stuck out his lip. 'My hat want its picture taken, too.'

'Please, Wombat,' said Mouse, stroking his ankle lovingly. So Wombat took off his hat, told it he wouldn't be long, and sat before the camera. He didn't like it at all. His back legs kept slipping from the chair, and his nose began to itch.

'Wombat, leave that nose alone!' ordered Tabby.

'It's my nose, you old cat,' said Wombat crossly.

'Please try and sit still,' said the photographer.

'Treely ruly I'm trying,' said Wombat. 'For you, Mouse,' he said.

At last all was ready. The photographer was hidden beneath his black cloth. Wombat was grumble-umbling to himself. Mouse

was waggling its ears so that Wombat would smile.

'No, no, there's some mud on his nose!' cried Tabby, and he dashed forward to brush it off just as the camera clicked.

'You wicked cat, you've spoiled the picture!' said the photographer. He was so upset that he wouldn't come out from under his black cloth. But Mouse sat on his shoe and argued. Mouse coaxed him to develop the picture so that they could have a look at it.

'Yes, I shall,' said the photographer, 'if you promise to go away and never come back. I'm not strong enough for wombats, really I'm not!'

The picture was a great surprise. It wasn't like Tabby, it wasn't like Wombat. There was Wombat's tubby form sitting on the chair. There was Tabby's catty little face on top of it. Yet somehow the Tabby face had short, stubby Wombat ears, and somehow the stout shape of Wombat had a long, grey catty tail.

'I shall never live down the shame!' said Tabby.

But Mouse entered the photograph in a funny pictures competition, and it won! It was called 'The Wonderful Womcat,' and won five pounds!

Tabby couldn't believe it.

Wombat couldn't believe it.

'It won't be long before we have our bike with red wheels!' said sensible Mouse.

Celeste Walters

WHO'S WHO
AT THE ZOO

ILLUSTRATED BY PATRICIA MULLINS

Opossum

O poss
I know why you are called
Opossum
it's 'cos that on bare heads you go
and drop your doings which we know
will make some people say 'Oh blow!'
and others say
'Oh possum!'

Beak Freak

The pelican will
keep fish in his bill
for it's better basted
before it is tasted.

Rachel Flynn

I HATE FRIDAYS

ILLUSTRATED BY CRAIG SMITH

Stories from Grade 4 kids at Koala Hills Primary School

NO NAUGHTY BOYS, PLEASE
BY THADEUS ANTWERP

I was looking forward to my birthday, and Mother said I could have some friends over for a barbecue. I thought I would invite eight, but Mother said two would be plenty, so we compromised and agreed on five.

Mother insisted that I invite some girls as she wasn't going to have a house full of boys. She said it is ridiculous to dislike girls as they make up half the population of the world, and she supposes I'll eventually marry one.

Then I composed the invitations. I asked David Pierce and Martin Peters, as well as Sally McKensie and Kerrie Street. However Martin couldn't come because his whole family would be out visiting relatives.

I couldn't invite any other boys because all the rest are naughty and Mother had said, 'NO NAUGHTY BOYS, PLEASE.' So I gave Martin's invitation to Kirsty Dean because . . . well . . . I quite like her.

On the day of the party there were three girls and two boys, including me.

My parents took us over to the park for the barbecue.

Father was going to play football with us while Mother cooked the sausages, BUT –

Kirsty was wearing a lace party frock.

Sally and Kerrie had brought their Barbie dolls.

David said he would prefer soccer.

And I find ball games distasteful.

So Father played soccer with David, I helped Mother with the cooking, and Kirsty looked very pretty.

Presently a brown dog arrived, apparently attracted by the smell of the sausages.

When lunch was ready we all had to stand ON the picnic table to keep away from the dog, who rather rudely put his head right into our esky and stole most of the bread.

Luckily it started to rain and we were able to pack up and go home.

Mother had made an excellent birthday cake the day before but the icing slid off during the night. So she piled a lot of pink jelly cakes onto a plate and stuck the candles into them.

It was adequate, but not quite what the children were expecting.

We finished off the afternoon with some spelling games. I'm afraid I won all of them.

My guests were really pleased when their parents came and got them.

I haven't been to any parties since then.

∽

CALL THAT A PARTY?

BY KERRIE STREET

THADEUS invited Sally and me to his birthday party. I didn't really want to go, but Mum and Dad said I should and that Thadeus is quite nice really.

Sally and I took our Barbie dolls in case there was nothing to play with. It's lucky we did, otherwise we would have had to play soccer with Mr Antwerp.

Kirsty Dean came. She was wearing a beautiful lace dress and had ribbons in her hair.

David Pierce was there because he's Thadeus's best friend.

We all went over to the park for a barbecue. It was awfully cold and windy.

As soon as the sausages were cooked a hungry dog came over. We had to stand right on top of the picnic table to keep away from it. Kirsty kept squealing and dropped her sausage on the ground. The dog grabbed it and ran right over our dolls where we had laid them down to sunbake.

Then it started raining and we had to pack up quickly and run back to the Antwerps' house.

Kirsty's curls had gone all stringy and she had sauce on her dress.

After we dried off, Mrs Antwerp brought out the birthday cake. You should have seen it. It was only a pile of jelly cakes with candles stuck in them.

Then we had some party games, but they were all spelling games, and Thadeus won every single one of them.

I was really glad when Dad came to get me.

We didn't even get a bag of lollies to take home.

Call that a party? I don't!

THE LOVE LETTER

BY DAVID PIERCE

THE other day after lunch, Thadeus found a letter in his desk. It said:

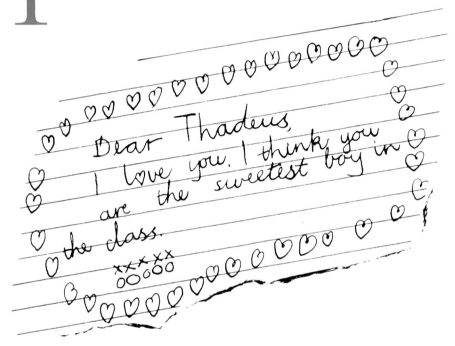

Dear Thadeus,
I love you. I think you
are the sweetest boy in
the class.
xxxxx
ooooo

There was no signature. We tried to guess who it was from.

Thadeus said he thought it might be from Kirsty because she went to his birthday party.

I said that it wouldn't be from Joan Smith or Josephine Wood because they both hate boys.

We didn't think it would be from Nancy Cleary because she can't write properly.

I walked around the room and looked at all the girls' handwriting, but none of it looked like the writing in the letter.

'Let's play a trick on Peter,' I said. 'Let's rub out your name and put in Peter's, and sign it "from Joan Smith".'

So we did.

I put the letter in Peter's desk while he was over at the bin sharpening his pencils. When he came back we both pretended to be very busy working.

He found the letter straight away and was sitting there slowly going pink, when Miss Finly said, 'What are you doing, Peter? You haven't done any work since lunchtime. I'll have that – ' and she took the letter out of his hand.

Peter stood up and sat down again and said, 'But – '

Then Miss Finly walked all around the room and checked everyone's writing. When she got to me she said, 'I want to see you when the bell goes.'

At playtime she told me that forgery was a crime and that I would have to apologise to Peter and to Joan and that she would keep the letter as evidence until I did.

Well she did, and I did and I never want to see another love-letter again – never ever.

∿

Morris Gleitzman and Paul Jennings

WICKED!

PART TWO

BATTERING RAMS

ILLUSTRATED BY DEAN GORISSEN

What had happened to the slimy slithering slobberers — and now the sheep? If only Dawn's new stepmother would believe her . . . If only Rory were there to back her up. But what had happened to him?

DAWN

I had something on my mind all the way back to the wrecker's yard.

Sheep.

I knew sheep pretty well, and I'd never seen them attack a person before. Not with a garden rake. Definitely not with a table fork.

What's going on? I wondered anxiously as I plodded along behind Eileen.

Were the sheep just grouchy because Ernie Piggot had upped and gone and left them?

Or were they out to get us like the slobberers?

A shiver of fear ran through me. I thought about the sheep on the tractor. Could sheep get a tractor started? I told myself to stop being dopey.

Then I realised Eileen had turned and was yelling at me. 'Stop dragging your feet,' she snapped. 'I want to get this charade over with. The sooner we knock this giant worm nonsense on the head, the sooner I can find out what's going on.'

She grabbed me by the arm and I had to trot to keep up with her. Then we both crashed to the ground.

There was a length of fencing wire stretched across the dirt track. As I tripped and fell forward I noticed something glinting in the dust. When my head cleared after the impact I saw what it was.

Glass. Jagged pieces of brown glass. Luckily I hadn't landed on any of them. Neither had Eileen. Having her arm in a sling had made her fall to one side. She lay on the grass verge, swearing.

Then I recognised a torn label on one of the pieces of glass. Sheep dip. We'd been tripped up so we'd cut ourselves on broken sheep-dip bottles.

I sat up in a panic and looked around. Sheep were watching us from each side of the track. I was just in time to see one of them open its mouth and drop an end of the fencing wire.

'Eileen.' My voice was a whisper. 'These sheep are out to get us.'

The sheep grinned menacingly.

'Bulldust,' yelled Eileen, struggling to her feet. She dragged me up. 'It's just kids playing stupid tricks, and if I catch them they'll suffer almost as much as you're going to. Now come on.'

She dragged me along the track. I glanced nervously over my shoulder. The sheep had gone. I was almost disappointed. If they whacked Eileen round the head with a fence post, then she'd know I wasn't a liar.

You'll see, I thought helplessly. When we get to the wrecker's yard and a hundred slobberers suck your innards out, then you'll see I was telling the truth.

At that moment I remembered I'd left my fence post back at Ernie Piggot's house. I tried to turn back, but Eileen's grip was unbreakable.

At least I had Mum's shoe inside my shirt.

I held it tight through the cloth. It made me feel better even though it wasn't much good as a weapon.

We were close to the wrecker's yard. I strained my ear for sounds of slobberers. My heart was pounding so loudly I couldn't hear much. Just some birds screeching and Eileen muttering about kids and their warped minds.

At the gate I stopped. 'Let's go to the police,' I pleaded. 'They can come and take photos of the slobberers and you can see those.'

Eileen looked at me grimly. 'If we're going to be a family, Dawn, we've got to start being honest with each other.'

She dragged me through the gate.

'No,' I yelled desperately. 'We don't stand a chance. They haven't eaten for hours. We'll be – '

I stopped and stared. The yard was empty. There wasn't a slobberer to be seen.

I tore my arm free and ran around the piles of scrap and the bus and the four-wheel drive and the big wrecker's crane, looking wildly.

Nothing.

'Okay, young lady,' yelled Eileen. 'Come here and start talking.'

I ignored her. I ran back to the bus and peered in, not caring if a tidal wave of slobberers poured out. At least then she'd know.

The bus was empty. Just the torn seats and the smashed speedometer and the goat's skeleton.

'Dawn,' roared Eileen.

Slowly I turned to face a life of not being believed and possibly being accused of killing and eating Rory.

Then I noticed something. On the ground. Big patches of what looked like cow poo. Dry and cracked. But not crumbly like cow poo. Hard like dried leather. When I kicked one I hurt my foot.

Of course. I remembered the slobberers' festering skins. They must have been dying. But what could have made them decompose so fast?

My thoughts were interrupted by Eileen grabbing me.

'I said,' she hissed, 'start talking.'

'They've died and shrivelled up,' I explained desperately. 'Look, you can see where they were. There and there and there and . . .'

'Cow dung,' said Eileen icily. 'It's dried cow dung, Dawn. Just like you're feeding me. Now tell me what's going on. Where's Rory?'

As I blinked back tears of rage and frustration, I was tempted to just make something up. 'He's run away from home because you're such a pain', something like that. But I knew Mum wouldn't have approved. She was a stickler for the truth. Even if it meant admitting she was five minutes late with the school bus because she'd got one of her uniform buttons jammed in my high chair.

'There's something weird and scary going on,' I said to Eileen. 'Maggots turning into bone-sucking monsters and sheep behaving in a very unfriendly manner. I don't know why and I don't know how, but it's happening.'

Eileen looked like she was going to explode.

She didn't. 'I shouldn't blame you,' she said, taking a deep breath. 'Not when your mother had so much trouble telling the truth.'

I felt like *I* was going to explode.

Before I could, I heard a loud creak above us. And a whoosh. I looked up. Swinging towards us was the big metal ball hanging from the end of the wrecker's crane.

Except it wasn't a ball of metal, it was a ball of sheep. About six of them, all with evil grins, clinging to the end of the chain.

I couldn't move. I stared horrified as the sheep hurtled towards us. Then I noticed something even worse. The sheep were glinting in the sun. Their wool wasn't soft and fluffy any more, it was hard and metallic.

Steel wool.

RORY

I ran screaming down the country road away from the remains of the dog. The glow of dawn and the morning mist meant nothing. My mind was a whirlpool of doubt, fear and horror. Was I mad? Did a goat's skeleton really come to life on that bus? Was Dawn's dead mother really there?

The whole thing was crazy, crazy, crazy. Even now slobberers could be waiting for me in the trees beside the road. Waiting to pounce and suck.

My bad leg ached. And my hand and arm were inflamed again. The purple bruise had spread. Pain filled my whole arm and part of my chest. Was my arm infected? The slobberers had licked me. Did I have some new illness? Slobberers' disease. Maybe I was dying.

I ran until I could run no further. I fell down exhausted in the middle of the road next to a slimy pond.

Eventually I got my breath back and sat up. I looked around me. All seemed quiet in the early morning light.

I still clutched the apple-man. I stared down at him. He was a bit grimy so I wiped him on my sleeve. I loved the apple-man.

He might have been the home of the slobberers. He might or might not have exploded on the bus. But he was still a gift from my dad. And even though he was an ugly little doll made out of a dried-up apple I was not going to part with him.

I think I knew, deep down inside me. Even way back then, at the beginning of it all. That the apple-man held the answers to all the questions I was too frightened to ask.

My feet stirred up the dust on the road as I slowly headed for home. Home? It wasn't really my place. Dawn's dad owned the house. And Dawn thought she owned it too. And Gramps, even though he was a nice guy and harmless, wasn't really *my* Gramps. Okay, Mum lived there now. But she always seemed to stick up for Dawn. Like that first time me and Mum went over to their place.

I don't know what all the fuss was about. Just because I made a double slingshot out of Dawn's bra. It could fire two tennis balls at once. Right over the house.

'Golf balls,' I told her. 'One on each side. That's all it would hold.'

Okay, so I lied a bit. And I ruined the bra. But Mum shouldn't have grounded me. Not her own son. Not her own flesh and blood.

I felt hurt. And angry. Really angry. And as I trudged along the road my arm hurt more and more. It was so painful that tears pricked behind my eyelids.

If only Dad were there. He would know what to do. He would know whether I was insane or not. He would stick up for me. He would help.

I looked down at the little apple-man with a bit of a smile and continued to force my aching legs towards the house. 'I'll show them,' I thought. 'You can't treat me like that.'

My arm and chest throbbed more and more. My bad leg

ached. I had to rest again. I sank down on a log, exhausted, and closed my eyes.

Something cold and wet moved across my hand. What, what, what? A slobberer's tongue? I was too scared to move. Too scared to open my eyes. But I had to.

Two eyes blinked back at me. Not a slobberer. Only a frog.

I laughed with relief and picked him up gently. 'Hello, little fella,' I said. The frog shot out his tiny tongue and tickled my cut hand. I could feel the small wet flick of it on the seeping scab of my wound. Suddenly the frog's eyes rolled back in his head and then quivered back into view. Like the symbols on a poker machine when you hit the jackpot.

The frog sat shivering on my palm. Why was it shivering? Frogs don't get cold, do they? Maybe it was scared. Like me.

Then the frog crouched. For a second it was like a coiled spring. Then its eyes rolled, and pow. It shot up into the sky with an enormous leap. Talk about the cow jumping over the moon. It disappeared over the top of the trees. *Splash*. It must have landed back in the pond.

What a jump. Incredible. I had never seen anything like it.

My mind started to tick over. The frog licking me. It reminded me of something. Something similar. What was it?

Then it clicked. The slobberers had licked my bleeding hand. And then there was the sheep. On the step of the bus. I had stuck my cut finger into the sheep's nostril.

Maybe there was some sort of disease going around. Maybe we were infecting each other. Like the Black Death. I needed help. I had to get home.

I staggered on down the road. On and on. It seemed such a long way home. Finally I reached the bridge. Not far now. I stopped and listened to the water gurgling below. And heard something else. Behind me in the bushes.

Plip, plop, plip, plop. Like tiny spoonfuls of jelly falling onto the road. Dozens of them. No, hundreds. *Plip, plop, plip, plop, plip, plop.* No, thousands. As if an unseen hand was throwing stones into the air.

There. Stretched across the road. Little green lumps with small blinking eyes. Suddenly they lifted into the air like a swarm of grasshoppers. Up, up, up, up. Way above the treetops. They stopped, paused in mid flight and began to fall. A hailstorm of frogs in the forest.

Whoosh, they landed together. As one. The sound reminded me of a huge bucket of water sloshing on the road. A million frogs, all landing at once.

They blinked at me. Unfriendly. My legs felt so weak I could hardly stand. But somehow I managed to back away from them across the bridge. Not for one second did I take my eyes off the fearful plague.

The frogs, as one, crouched down and then sprang. Way, way over my head. Right across the river in one – no, not one. But one million identical giant leaps. They sloshed down onto the road and jumped again. And again.

The shower of frogs disappeared into the distance along the dusty road.

Towards our house.

I stumbled after them as fast as I could go. I was nearly there.

Home at last. Suddenly it all seemed silly. A nightmare. Unreal. There were no frogs. It was all a mistake. All my tiredness fell away. Even my arm didn't hurt quite as much as I trudged the last few steps up to the gate. Now I could get adult help. They could take over.

Slobberers, a skeleton goat, Dawn's mother back from the dead, an exploding apple-man and frogs that can jump trees. They were all just in my head. Part of my sickness. None of that would matter any more.

A shadowy figure moved in the kitchen window. Mum? Maybe Mum was there by now. And Jack. Oh, I hoped so much that they were. I let out a sob and opened the gate.

A thunderous roar filled the air. It was almost as if the movement of the gate had been a signal for it to start. I clapped my hands over my ears and started running for the front door. What *was* that noise? So loud.

It was an ordinary old noise made bigger. A noise from a peaceful morning in the country. But amplified like a rock band out of control.

Frogs. A billion frogs croaking together. I couldn't see them but there was no doubt that they were there. Hiding in the trees that surrounded the house.

Kevin Gilbert

ME AND MARY KANGAROO

PHOTOGRAPHS BY ELEANOR WILLIAMS

'The memory I love the most is when I was a little boy and used to play with my friend, Mary Kangaroo.'

WHEN I was a little boy there was no such thing as a supermarket or an ice-cream parlour. We lived four miles away from town, out along the Old Forbes Road toward the Sandhills, over Chinaman's Bridge and past the weir on the Goobang Creek, a tributary of the Lachlan River. It was full of yellowbelly bream and yabbies, ducks and swans, blue cranes, black and white ibis and water rats.

We had no close neighbours and could see for miles around because there were no houses, no trees, only some briar berry bushes on the plains. Our ice-cream came via a pretty, coloured ice-cream cart driven by the ice-cream man,

Bung-eye Naden, who was also my cousin. He was called 'Bung-eye' because the flies were something dreadful in our country and they'd sting our eyes and make them swell up. We think Bung-eye went into the ice-cream-selling business because he ran foul of the flies and had some bother with his eyes. He was the nicest friend we had, apart from our mum and dad. Mary Kangaroo could always tell when Bung-eye was coming, long before I heard his ice-cream bell over the plains. You'd swear she had pains, prancing and wriggling and *tcha-tcha-tcha* clicking-talking. If she'd been a parrot she'd have screeched or started squawking like a hen, I think, but I knew what she was saying. Mum would give us two pennies and we'd skip, breathless, a mile over the hot dust for an ice-cream that could never last the distance home in that heat. Although I must admit that the ice-cream was never given the chance to get warm before disappearing in a thousand quick licks.

Bung-eye blared out 'Greensleeves' music and jangled his big brass bell. He always said, with a big happy teasing toss of his head, 'Hello, Darlin'. What can I do for you?' and 'Hi there, Mary Kangaroo.'

I would say politely, 'Hello, Bung-eye. It's a lovely day. One for me and one for Mary, too, please.' If we were *real* lucky – and more often than not we were *real, real* lucky – Bung-eye would give us a red-and-white-striped bullseye lolly each and sometimes a sherbert, with licorice, to share. His horse, old roan-coloured Tibby, always gave a snicker of 'How do you do, you two?' to me and Mary Kangaroo. We would give her a stroke on her muzzle and Mary would sniff up to her nostril. Tibby would chomple at Mary with her lips.

Sometimes I'd be naughty. I'd let my ice-cream fall out of its cone into the dust, groan a bellow-cry and yell, all sobs, and moan, I would. Bung-eye, being kind and good, always understood and couldn't drive away leaving a little boy and a small kangaroo alone, so far from home, crying fit to burst and flood the Lachlan River with tears. So he'd say, 'Don't cry, Darlin'. Here's another ice-cream. Quick, Darlin', take it, eat it, before *I* scream! This time

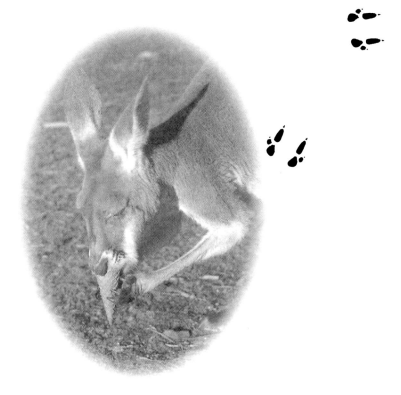

I'll press it into the cone harder.' Before you could say 'Hooray', my tears dried up and Bung-eye rang the bell for Tibby, 'Up and go, the other children are waiting for us. Goodbye, Darlin'. Goodbye, Mary Kangaroo.'

He never stopped to see what we used to do. We'd carefully dust off the ice-cream that dropped, so we could lick and share as we skipped and hopped for home.

∾

Ethel Turner

SEVEN LITTLE AUSTRALIANS

COLOUR ILLUSTRATIONS BY JOHN LENNOX
AND BETINA OGDEN

Bunty was a great storyteller, who could only be kept in check by his older sister Judy. But Judy had been sent to boarding school in disgrace.

BUNTY had been betrayed into telling another story. It was a very big one, and he was proportionately miserable. Everyone else had gone out but Meg, who was still in bed after her fainting-fit, and he had been having a lonely game of cricket down in the paddock by himself. But even with a brand-new cricket ball this game palls after a time when one has to bowl and bat and backstop in solitary state. So presently he put his bat over into the garden, and began to throw the ball about in an aimless fashion, while he cogitated on what he should do next. His father's hack was standing away at the farther end of the paddock, and in an idle, thoughtless way Bunty sauntered down towards it, and then sent his ball spinning over the ground in its direction 'to give it a jump'. Nothing was further from his thoughts than an idea of hurting the animal, and when the ball struck it full on the leg, and it moved away limping, he hastened down to it, white and anxious.

He could see he had done serious mischief by the way the poor thing held its leg up from the ground and quivered when he touched it. Terror seized him forthwith, and he turned hastily round with his usual idea of hiding in his head. But to his utter dismay, when he got half way back across the paddock he saw his father and a brother officer come out of the wicket gate leading from the garden and saunter slowly down in the direction of the horse, which was a valuable and beautiful one.

In terror at what he had done, he slipped the cricket ball into the front of his sailor jacket, and, falling hurriedly upon his knees, began playing an absorbing game of marbles. His trembling thumb had hit about a dozen at random when he heard his name called in stentorian tones.

He rose, brushed the dust from his shaking knees, and walked slowly down to his father.

'Go and tell Pat I want him instantly,' the Captain said. He had the horse's leg in his hand and was examining it anxiously. 'If he's not about, send Pip. I can't think how it's happened – do you know anything of this, Bunty?'

'No, of course not! I n-never did n-n-nothing,' Bunty said with chattering teeth, but his father was too occupied to notice his evident guilt, and bade him go at once.

So he went up to the stables and sent Pat post-haste back to his father.

And then he stole into the house, purloined two apples and a bit of cake from the dining room, and went away to be utterly miserable until he had confessed.

He crept into a disused shed some distance from the house. In days gone by it had been a stable, and had a double loft over it that was only to be reached by a ladder in the last stage of dilapidation. Bunty scrambled up, sat down in an unhappy little heap among some straw, and began thoughtfully to gnaw an apple.

If ever a little lad was in need of a wise, loving, motherly mother it was this same dirty-faced, heavy-hearted one who sat with his small rough head against a cobwebby beam and muttered dejectedly, ' 'Twasn't my fault. 'Twas the horse.'

He fancied something moved in the second loft, which was divided from the one he was in by a low partition. 'Shoo, shoo, get away!' he called, thinking it was rats. He struck the floor several times with his heavy little boots.

'Shoo!' he said.

'Bunty.'

The boy turned pale to his lips. That odd, low whisper of his name, that strange rustle so near him – what *could* it mean?

'Bunty.'

Again the name sounded. Louder this time, but in a tired voice, that struck him some way with a strange thrill. The rustling grew louder, something was getting over the partition, crossing the floor, coming towards him. He gave a sob of terror and flung himself face downwards on the ground, hiding his little blanched face among the straw.

'Bunty,' said the voice again, and a light hand touched his arm.

'Help me – *help* me!' he shrieked. 'Meg – oh! Father – Esther!'

But one hand was hastily put over his mouth and another pulled him into a sitting position.

He had shut his eyes very tightly, so as not to see the ghostly visitant that he knew had come to punish him for his sin. But something made him open them, and then he felt he could never close them again for amazement.

For it was Judy's hand that was over his mouth, and Judy's self that was standing beside him.

'My golly!' he said, in a tone of stupefaction. He stared at her to make sure she was real flesh and blood. 'How*ever* did you get here?' But Judy made no answer. She merely took the remaining apple and cake from his hand, and, sitting down, devoured them in silence.

'Haven't you got any more?' she said anxiously.

Then he noticed what a tall, gaunt, strange-looking Judy it was. Her clothes were hanging round her almost in tatters, her boots were burst and white with dust, her brown face was thin and sharp, and her hair matted and rough.

'My golly!' the little boy said again, his eyes threatening to start out of his head. 'My golly, Judy, what have you been doin'?'

'I – I've run away, Bunty,' Judy said, in a quavering voice. 'I've walked all the way from school. I wanted to see you all so badly.'

'My jiggery!' Bunty said.

'I've thought it all out,' Judy continued, pushing back her hair in a weary way. 'I can't quite remember everything just now, I am so tired, but everything will be all right.'

'But what'll he say?' Bunty said with frightened eyes, as a vision of his father crossed his mind.

'He won't know, of course,' Judy returned, in a matter-of-fact manner. 'I shall just live here in this loft for a time, and you can all come to see me and bring me food and things, and then presently I'll go back to school.' She sank down among the straw and shut her eyes in an exhausted way for a minute or two, and Bunty watched her half fascinated.

'How far is it from your school?' he said at last.

'Seventy-seven miles.' Judy shuddered a little. 'I got a lift in a luggage train from Lawson to Springwood, and a ride in a cart for a little way, but I walked the rest. I've been nearly a week coming,' she added after a pause, and shut her eyes again for quite a long time. Then a tear or two of weakness and self-pity trickled from beneath her black lashes, and made a little clean mark down her cheeks. Bunty's throat swelled at the sight of them, he had never seen Judy cry as long as he could remember. He patted her thin hand, he rubbed his head against her shoulder, and said, 'Never mind, old girl', in a thick voice.

But that brought half a dozen great heavy drops hurrying down from beneath the closed lashes, and the girl turned over and lay face downwards to hide them. Then she struggled up to a sitting position and actually began to laugh.

'*If* the Miss Burtons could see me!' she said. 'Oh, I've managed everything *so* beautifully. They think I'm spending a fortnight at Katoomba – oh, *Bunty*, you ought to see the curls Miss Marian Burton wears plastered to each side of her cheeks!' She broke off, laughing almost hysterically, and then coughing till the tears came back in her eyes.

'Do go and get me something to eat,' she said crossly, when she got her breath. 'You might remember I've had nothing to eat since yesterday morning – only you always were selfish, Bunty.'

He got up and moved away in a great hurry. 'What could you eat? What shall I get?' he said, and put one leg down the trap door.

'Anything so long as it's a lot,' she said. '*Anything!* I feel I could eat this straw, and crunch up the beams as if they were biscuits. I declare I've had to keep my eyes off you, Bunty, you're so fat I keep longing to pick your bones.'

Her eyes shone with a spark of their old fun, but then she began to cough again, and, after the paroxysm had passed, lay back exhausted.

'Do fetch some of the others,' she called faintly, as his head was disappearing. 'You're not much good alone, you know.'

His head bobbed back a moment, and he tried to smile away the pain her words gave him, for just at that minute he would have died for her without a murmur.

'I'm awf'ly sorry, Judy,' he said gently, 'but the others are all out. Wouldn't I do? I'd do anything, Judy – please.'

Judy disregarded the little sniffle that accompanied the last words, and turned her face to the wall.

Two big tears trickled down again.

'They *might* have stayed in,' she said with a sob. 'They might have known I should try to come. Where are they?'

'Pip's gone fishing,' he said, 'and Nell's carrying the basket for him. And Baby's at the Courtneys', and Esther's gone to town with the General. Oh, and Meg's ill in bed, because her stays were too tight last night and she fainted.'

'I suppose they haven't missed me a scrap,' was her bitter thought, when she heard how everything seemed to be going on as usual, while she had been living through so much just to see them all.

Then the odd feeling of faintness came back, and she closed her eyes again and lay motionless, forgetful of time, place, or hunger.

Bunty sped across the paddock on winged feet – the sight of his father near the stables gave him a momentary shock, and brought his own trouble to mind, but he shook it off again and hurried on.

The pantry door was locked. Martha, the cook, kept it in that condition generally on account of his own sinful propensities for making away with her tarts and cakes – it was only by skilful stratagem he could ever get in, as he remembered dejectedly.

But Judy's hunger! Nothing to eat since yesterday morning!

He remembered, with a feeling of pain even now, the horrible sinking sensation he had experienced last week when for punishment he had been sent to bed without his tea. And Judy had forgone three meals! He shut his lips tightly, and a light of almost heroic resolve came into his eyes. Round at the side of the house was the window to the pantry – he had often gazed longingly up at it, but had never ventured to attempt the ascent, for there was a horrible cactus creeper up the wall.

But now for Judy's sake he would do it or die.

He marched round the house and up to the side window. No one was about, the whole place seemed very quiet. Martha, as he had seen, was cooking in the kitchen, and the other girl was whitening the front verandah. He gave one steady look at the great spiky thorns, and the next minute was climbing up among them.

Oh, how they pierced and tore him! There was a great jagged wound up one arm, his left stocking was ripped away and a deep red scratch showed across his leg, his hands were bleeding and quivering with pain.

But he had reached the sill, and that was everything.

He pushed up the narrow window, and with much difficulty forced his little fat body through. Then he dropped down on to a shelf, and lowered himself gingerly on to the floor. There was no time to stay to look at his many hurts, he merely regarded the biggest scratch with rueful eyes, and then began to look around for provender. The pantry was remarkably empty – not a sign of cakes, not a bit of jelly, not a remnant of fowl anywhere. He cut a great piece off a loaf, and carefully wrapped some butter in a scrap of newspaper. There was some corned beef on a dish, and he cut off a thick lump and rolled it up with the remains of a loquat tart. These parcels he disposed of down the loose front of his sailor coat, filling up his pockets with sultanas, citron-peel, currants, and such dainties as the store bottles held. And then he prepared to make his painful retreat.

He climbed upon the shelf once more, put his head out of the window, and gave a look of despair at the cactus. And even as he knelt there sounded behind him the sharp click of a turning key.

He looked wildly round, and there was Martha in the doorway, and to his utter horror she was talking to his father, who was in the passage just beyond.

'Row's Embrocation, or arnica,' the Captain was saying. 'It is probably in this pantry, my good girl, because it is the last place I should expect it to be in. I left it on my bedroom mantelpiece, but somebody has seen fit to meddle with it. Why in the name of all that is mysterious can't you let my things alone?'

'And for what should I be after moving it for?' Martha retorted. 'I don't mix the pastry with it to make it lightsome, leastway not ordinarily.'

She tossed her head, and the action revealed the small, kneeling, terrified figure at the window.

Now the door was only half-open, and her master was standing just beside it outside, so she only had the benefit of the spectacle.

Twice she opened her mouth to speak, but Bunty made such frantic, imploring faces at her that she closed it again, and even began to examine the bottles on the shelf near the door to give the boy an opportunity of retreat.

One minute and he would have been safe – one minute and he would have been in the thick of the cactus, that had quite lost its terrors.

But the Fates were too strong for him. And all because Martha Tomlinson's shoe was down at the heel. In turning round it twisted a little under her, and, in trying to recover her balance, she put out one hand. And in putting out one hand she knocked over a jug. And the jug communicated its shock to a dish, which toppled over, and coolly pushed the great basin of milk off the shelf on to the floor. I don't know if ever you have tried to clean a board floor after milk, but I am sure you can imagine it would be a disagreeable task – especially if you had scrubbed it well only that morning. It was hardly to be wondered at, therefore, that Martha, in her profound irritation at the disaster, turned angrily round, and, pointing to the figure now stuck in the window, demanded in an exasperated tone whether the blessed saints could stand that dratted boy any longer, for she couldn't, so there.

The Captain took an angry step into the pantry and gave a roar of command for Bunty to come down.

The boy dropped in an agony of dread and shrinking.

'Always his hands a–pickin' and stealin' and his tongue a–lyin',' said Martha Tomlinson, gazing unkindly at the unhappy child.

Two, three, four, five angry cuts from the riding whip in the Captain's hands, and Bunty had ducked under his arm and fled howling down the passage and out of the back door.

Away across the paddocks he went, sobbing at every step, but hugely commending himself for bearing all this for someone else's sake.

He could hardly have believed, had anyone told him previously, that he could have done anything so absolutely noble, and the thought comforted him even while the cuts and scratches smarted. He tried to stifle his sobs as he reached the shed, and even stuffed half a handful of currants into his mouth towards that end.

But it was a very tearful, scratched, miserable face that bobbed up the opening near Judy again.

She did not move, though her eyes were half-open, and he knelt down and shook her shoulder gently.

'Here's some things, Judy – ain't you goin' to eat them?'

She shook her head very slightly.

'Have some corned beef, or some currants – there's some peel, too, if you'd rather.'

She shook her head again. 'Do take them away,' she said, with a little moan.

A look of blank disappointment stole over his small, heated face.

'An' I've half killed myself to get them! Well, you *are* a mean girl!' he said.

'Oh *do* go away,' Judy moaned, moving her head restlessly from side to side. 'Oh, how my feet ache! No – my head, and my side – oh! I don't know what it is!'

'I got hit here and here,' Bunty said, indicating the places, and wiping away tears of keen self-pity with his coat sleeve. 'I'm scratched all over with that beastly old cactus.'

'Do you suppose there are many miles more?' Judy said, in such a quick way that all the words seemed to run into each other. 'I've walked hundreds and hundreds, and haven't got home yet. I suppose it's because the world's round, and I'll be walking in at the school gate again presently.'

'Don't be an idjut!' Bunty said gruffly.

'You'll be sure and certain, Marian, never to breathe a word of it. I've trusted you, and if you keep faith I can go home and come back and no one will know. And lend me two shillings, can you? I've not got much left. Bunty, you selfish little pig, you might get me some milk! I've been begging and begging of you for hours, and my head is going to Catherine wheels for want of it.'

'Have some corned beef, Judy, dear – oh, Judy, don't be so silly and horrid after I nearly got killed for you,' Bunty said, trying with trembling fingers to stuff a piece into her mouth.

The little girl rolled over and began muttering again.

'Seventy-seven miles,' she said, 'and I walked eleven yesterday, that makes eleven hundred and seventy-seven – and six the day before because my foot had a blister – that's eleven hundred and eighty-three. And if I walk ten miles a day I shall get home in eleven hundred and eighty-three times ten, that's a thousand and – oh! What is it? Whatever is it? Bunty, you horrid little pig, can't you tell me what it is? My head aches too much to work, and a thousand and something days – that's a year – two years – two years – three years before I get there. Oh, Pip, Meg, three years! Oh, Esther! Ask him, ask him to let me come home! Three years – years – years!'

The last word was almost shrieked and the child struggled to her feet and tried to walk.

Bunty caught her arms and held her. 'Let me go, can't you?' she said hoarsely. 'I shall never get there at this rate. Three years, and all those miles!'

She pushed him aside and tried to walk across the loft, but her legs tottered under her and she fell down in a little senseless heap. 'Meg – I'll fetch Meg,' said the little boy in a trembling, alarmed voice, and he slipped down the opening and hastened up to the house.

∽

Robin Klein

HATING
ALISON ASHLEY

COLOUR ILLUSTRATIONS BY NIGEL BUCHANAN AND BETINA OGDEN

BLACK AND WHITE ILLUSTRATION BY BETINA OGDEN

*Erica Yurken felt superior to everyone at notorious Barringa East, until
Alison Ashley – beautiful, rich and clever – unexpectedly turned up.*

W E didn't speak to each other for a whole week. Every day she wore something new to school and every day her work folder collected A's and flattering comments from Miss Belmont. All the teachers doted on her in a very sickening manner. At assembly they'd be hectoring their classes into what passed for straight lines at Barringa East Primary, and they'd turn and look at Alison Ashley standing there as polite and nicely brought up as a nativity angel, and their eyes would glimmer with faint hope for the human race. Maybe they thought that Alison's excellent qualities would spread around the whole school and infect everyone, like gastro-enteritis.

But it was peculiar, because none of the other kids took to

124

NIGEL BUCHANAN

her at all. She was just so private and never started conversations or yakked on about herself. So everyone sort of skated warily around her, not stirring her, because kids who were that pretty and that well dressed didn't get stirred. But they acted as though she didn't really belong to our school at all, as though she was just a visitor.

The same way they treated me.

The tension between Alison Ashley and myself caused us to sit as far apart as possible from each other in class. If her work slid over to my side of the desk, I shoved it right back, and if any of my lunch crumbs got over on her side, she'd shovel them back with her ruler, as though they'd been sprayed with poisonous toxins.

With this cold war going on between us, you wouldn't have supposed for one minute that she'd turn up uninvited at my house and get herself asked for tea.

This is how it happened.

It was late Friday afternoon. Lennie was at the kitchen table, back from Wollongong, or wherever he'd been with his old truck, and he was not only sitting at our table, but Mum was sitting on his knee. I found that extremely embarrassing. She was much too old in my opinion to have a boyfriend, anyhow. Not that Lennie was my idea of anyone's boyfriend, with his bald patch and his feeble jokes that were about a million years old. (Such as if Valjoy asked Mum for money for the pictures and Mum said, 'Try and get in for half, love,' Lennie would be bound to say, 'Which half of you wants to go?')

'I thought I told you not to wear my silver slave bangles to school?' Valjoy said when I came in. (Every time Valjoy and I met, she began conversations with that phrase: I thought I told you.)

'Erk can be my slave girl any old tick of the clock,' said Lennie. 'Come on, Erk, do us a belly dance. What's the good of wanting to go on the stage if you can't do a spot of belly dancing?' (That shows you the level of his conversation.)

'We're having a barbecue tonight, Erk,' Mum said. 'And Len's shouting us to the drive-in after.'

'Are we supposed to be going in Lennie's truck? If so, I'm not coming. What if I saw anyone I knew there?'

'So what if you did?' demanded Mum. 'Honest, Erk, you're getting that sour and critical lately. You never have a nice word to say to anyone in this house. It'll do you good, madam, starting at Barringa High next year and have your head flushed in the toilet.'

'That's a complete myth,' I said. 'Anyhow, I'd kill anyone who tried to flush my head in a toilet.'

'That's the goods,' Lennie said. 'I like a slave girl with a bit of spirit.'

I didn't answer him, because if there was one thing Lennie didn't need, it was encouragement. I cleared a space on the kitchen table to mix up some lemon cordial. This is what I had to clear away: a library book about astral projection; a pair of fake eyelashes; three empty beer cans; a black lace bra; a million horse swapcards; the *Turf Guide*; a plastic tub of shop-made potato salad that had been left out of the fridge and now sprouted a topping of penicillin; a bottle of shoe dye; and the cat. Our cat was a black tom called Norm with a horrible nature, and he swivelled around and bit me on the wrist.

There wasn't a scrap of gracious living at our house.

The doorbell rang. I didn't bother to get up and answer it, because the last four times when I did, it was to see the back view of Barry Hollis nicking off down the street.

'I'll get it,' said Valjoy. 'I'm expecting Spider and Blonk and Poison. We're going round to Macker's house to see his Suzuki.'

'If Spider's the one with the head like a hard-boiled egg sliced off at the top, and the python tatto, and the safety pin through his ear, I don't want you asking him in, Valjoy,' Mum said strictly.

'Last time he was here, he washed his leather jacket in the sink without even asking first.'

I sipped moodily at my lemon cordial through a straw. At least using a straw can give you a feeling of refined living, although it can't be compared to drinking champagne out of a crystal glass with a stem.

Valjoy yelled from the hall, 'Mum, tell Blonk and Poison when they come that we've gone round to Macker's anyway. And Erk, here's a kid from your school wants to see you, can't think why.'

I looked up, and there was Alison Ashley in our kitchen.

I would, from humiliation, have trickled down under the table and stayed there for ever, but the area under our table was pretty crowded. As well as people's legs, there was this huge stockpile of ironing, and the vacuum cleaner, and a half-built stable complex belonging to Jedda.

'Hullo, love,' said Mum to Alison Ashley. 'You in the same class as Erk?'

'I took home Erica's pencil case by mistake, Mrs Yurken,' Alison said, so politely. 'I thought I'd better return it because of all the homework we've got to do over the weekend. I'm sorry, I guess I must have picked it up accidentally with my things.' She put my pencil case down on the table next to Valjoy's black lace bra and the false eyelashes.

My pencil case wasn't a proper one. It was just a cardboard box decorated with ballerina pictures, drawn by me. I noticed with mortification that I'd drawn all the ballet shoes with dozens of straps crossing over and over.

'Hey, sweetheart, you're a good looker,' Lennie said to Alison. 'Reckon I'll go back to school. Fillies didn't look like you when I was at school.'

(I personally didn't believe that Lennie ever went to school at all. I think he just groped his way out of a forest covered in bark and lichen like something out of a science-fiction story.)

'Say thank you about the pencil case, Erk,' Mum said. 'Where's your manners?'

'Thanks,' I muttered into my lemon-flavoured junk food.

'Tell you what, love,' Mum said to Alison. 'We're having a barbecue. So why don't you stay and have tea with us?'

I prayed for Lennie to swallow the flip top off his beer can and have to be rushed to hospital. I concentrated on sending Mum ESP messages all screaming out NO! But my mum was abnormally sociable, and you could tell she was thrilled to bits that finally some kid from school was dropping in at our house.

I hurled ESP messages at Alison Ashley screaming, 'Don't you dare stay here! I don't want you! Get back to Hedge End Road where you belong!'

But all Alison said was, 'Thank you very much for the invitation, Mrs Yurken. There's no need to ring my mother. She'll be working late tonight, so I was home by myself anyhow. I'm sure she wouldn't mind if I stayed, as long as I get home before dark.'

I could have died.

'You and Erk might want to play records in her room till tea's ready,' said Mum. 'Erk's just mad about that group Splunge, or Splurge or whatever they're called. She's got their album. Plays it non-stop.'

I really could have died.

Splurge was a group all the little kids in grade five and younger raved about, and I certainly didn't wish to advertise to Alison Ashley of all people that I owned their album. I dragged myself numbly up the hall, with her following, and hesitated at the door of my bedroom. I thought of the horrific mess Jedda's side was in. She'd set up some carton steeple chase hurdles down the middle of the room, and her mattress and bedding were rolled up on the floor. I kept telling her that she'd grow up all twisted like an espalier fruit tree if she slept there, but she never took any notice of me, maybe because I didn't look like a racehorse trainer.

I couldn't invite Alison Ashley into that weird-looking room. So I opened the door of Valjoy's and said, 'This is my room.'

Valjoy had a weekend job at the milkbar, and she spent all the money left over from buying clothes on interior decorating. She'd painted the walls black and the ceiling gold, and a huge stereo, which Blonk gave her for her fifteenth birthday, took up almost one wall. Mum wasn't too happy about having it in the house, because she said Blonk certainly couldn't have afforded such an expensive set by legal means. Sometimes when the police sirens were wailing up and down Wilga Street late at night after the Eastside Boys, Mum became nervous enough to unscrew the handle off Valjoy's bedroom door, so if the police accused her of harbouring stolen property, they couldn't get at the evidence in a hurry.

Valjoy had a fake leopard-fur bedspread, a pink plush elephant the size of Lennie, and a yellow bean bag. I sprawled casually on the leopard-skin bedspread. 'You can look through my record

collection if you like,' I said. 'That's not really true, what Mum said about me liking Splurge. You know how parents get things wrong. My little sister is the one who's rapt in Splurge.'

Alison inspected Valjoy's vast collection of albums. Valjoy used to go with this boy who worked in a record shop, and he was always giving her records which he got at a discount. Or more likely pinched.

'It's a pity, but I can't play any for you right now,' I said. 'The stereo needs a new needle. I'm terribly fussy about scratching my records.' The truth was that I didn't know how to work Valjoy's record player, which had as many dials and knobs as an intensive-care unit. Also, she'd said she'd paralyse me if she caught me anywhere near it. 'You can look at my clothes if you want to,' I said. 'Just slide open the wardrobe doors.'

Alison didn't say anything, but she riffled along the long line of coathangers. Valjoy had thirteen pairs of jeans and twice that many tops, and a pair of shiny fake-leather pants, and a lot of dresses Mum wouldn't let her wear in public unless she put a cardigan on over the top.

'Are you allowed to wear high heels?' Alison asked.

Valjoy had all these pairs of strappy shoes with heels as high as lighthouses. 'Of course I'm allowed to,' I said.

'How come you never wear any of these clothes to school?' Alison asked.

'I save them for the Cascade Disco on Saturday nights.'

'Are you really allowed to go to that place?'

'That's what I use all that make up for,' I said, waving airily at Valjoy's dressing table. Valjoy knew a boy whose mother was an Avon lady, and she was always receiving gifts of cosmetics, though Mum said that the boy's mother must wonder why her stocks were always running low.

'You can try on any of that make-up,' I said. 'I've got plenty. Help yourself to some of that blue eyeshadow with the glittery stuff in it.'

'I don't think I'd better,' said Alison Ashley. 'I'm not allowed to wear make up. My mother would be cross.'

My mother would be cross! Honestly! Everyone else I knew would say, 'Mum would chuck a mental,' or, 'I'd get a clip over the ear.'

Alison sat down in the bean bag. I'd always thought that there was no possible way anyone, even the Queen, could plonk down into a beanbag and still look dignified. But Alison Ashley managed to. One minute she was standing up looking at Valjoy's warpaint, and the next she was sitting gracefully in that beanbag with her ankles crossed and her hands folded neatly in her lap.

I picked up one of Valjoy's glossy magazines and flipped through the pages. When I came to the centrefold I was embarrassed and quickly put the magazine back.

'I guess you've done all that homework already?' I said crossly.

'I haven't even thought about the homework yet,' Alison said. 'I'm not all that interested in homework. I did marsupials in grade four, anyhow.'

'Miss Belmont is a fantastic teacher.'

'I never said she wasn't.'

'Everyone does their homework in her class. Even Barry Hollis always turns in something, even if it's just a couple of sentences.

We're lucky to have her for our grade teacher.'

Alison Ashley didn't say anything for a long time. Vanquished.

'Was that your dad out there in the kitchen?' she asked, changing the subject.

'Certainly not!' I said indignantly. I considered various ways I could explain Lennie. I could say Mum was a psychiatrist and Lennie one of her patients. Or that he was our gardener, only that would have sounded peculiar because our front yard was so primitive.

'I thought he must be your dad because your mother was sitting on his knee,' Alison said.

Could I say Lennie was my grandfather? She'd never believe that, because he didn't look quite that old enough, and ladies my mum's age probably didn't go round sitting on their father's knee, anyhow.

'He's a friend of hers,' I said sulkily. 'But she doesn't really like him. He's not her boyfriend or anything like that. Her real boyfriend's fantastic. He's very handsome and he owns a racehorse stud-farm and a Mercedes. He's going to buy Mum a fur coat the day she agrees to marry him. I help train the racehorses at that place he has.'

'Really?'

'I just said so, didn't I? My real father is dead.'

'Oh,' said Alison. 'Sorry.'

My real dad wasn't dead at all. Last thing we heard was that he was wanted in Queensland for selling shares in a non-existent tin mine.

'My father was killed in a plane crash,' I said. 'He was a test pilot. When he knew the plane was going to crash, he flew out over the ocean and crashed there so he wouldn't come down on any houses. Every year on the anniversary of his death, I take a big wreath of roses down to the beach and cast it out to the tide. But you'd better not mention to my mum that I told you about my father getting killed. She never got over it.'

'But I thought you said she had a boyfriend with a racehorse stud-farm now?'

'What's that got to do with it?' I demanded. 'My mum's very popular. She's a hotel manageress. They have big wedding receptions there. When they get really busy, I help out. I wear a black dress and black high heels and a little white frilly apron and serve pre-dinner drinks to the customers.'

'Oh,' said Alison Ashley.

Her face never seemed to reflect moods at all like normal faces. You just couldn't tell what she was thinking deep down in those Royal Show Blue Ribbon eyes. She made me feel nervous, and when I felt nervous I always talked a lot to cover up.

'We're only living in Barringa East because my brother is training to be a missionary,' I said. 'He works amongst socially disadvantaged people. He's a monk, only while he's away from his monastery, he doesn't wear that brown dressing-gown thing that monks on TV usually do. He has special permission to wear jeans. Only you mustn't tell anyone I told you about Harley, because they have to take a vow of secrecy, all those monks.'

'Oh,' said Alison Ashley.

'So we're only renting this house until Harley finishes his missionary training,' I said. 'Our real house is in that suburb where

Kyle Grammar School is. That's where we really live. But it's all shut up now, with a cover over the heated inground swimming pool. Lennie, the man you saw out in the kitchen, he's a private security guard. He just came over here to tell Mum he checked up on our other house to see no one's broken into it while we're living in Barringa East so Harley can dedicate his life to the poor.'

'Erk!' yelled Jedda. 'Mum says the barbecue's ready and you and that other girl got to come out now.'

She banged open the door of Valjoy's room and glanced at Alison, only without much interest because Alison had Roman sandals on instead of hooves. 'What are you doing in Valjoy's . . . ' she began, but I shot up and pushed her out into the hall. 'Come and see my new stable bed I made,' she said, grabbing Alison's hand. 'You can crawl in and have a sleep if you like.'

I hastily snatched Alison's other hand and tugged her towards the kitchen. It was like one of those scenes where they tie a victim to four wild horses to get the truth out of them, only I think Alison would have managed to look poised and graceful even if that was happening to her.

But Jedda shoved open the door of our room, and I could have died. There was the usual revolting sight of all her weekly snacks on the floor next to the hooped-up mattress. And since she wasn't using her bed to sleep in, she'd dumped every single toy and article of clothing she owned on the wire base. She said it was quicker than hunting for things through the chest of drawers. Disorder, chaos, shame and utter mortification.

Alison Ashley looked at Jedda's part of the room and blinked incredulously. Then she glanced at my bed. There was the red tracksuit top I wore to school most days slung over one bed post, and my school bag over the other. And my Barringa East Primary School gym skirt and top lying on the spread. Also my Splurge album with my name on it in big purple texta letters.

'I sleep in this room sometimes because Jedda gets bad dreams,' I said. 'When she was a baby she was trapped in a burning pram for several hours before being rescued.'

'Was I?' asked Jedda with interest.

'Tea, I mean dinner, is ready,' I said quickly.

The barbecue was really terrible. I died every few minutes. It seemed to me that every person in our family was trying their hardest to act and sound and look like people who lived in caves, to show me up in front of Alison Ashley.

Jedda handed her a sausage. Just a sausage by itself, with no plate or fork or anything, and Alison looked at it and said politely, 'Could I have a paper tissue, please?'

Lennie shook up a can of Coke and squirted Mum with it, and she squirted him back with the hose. Our cat jumped on the barbecue (he wasn't scared of anything, even fire), grabbed a steak and snarled and flexed his claws when Lennie tried to make him give it back. Mum yelled out to Harley that the food was getting cold, and he strolled out of his bungalow wearing underpants which had a pattern of red ants on a black background. I thought gloomily that even Alison Ashley wouldn't believe that any monastery would let him wear clothes like that.

'Harley,' scolded Mum. 'Get back in there and put some jeans or a towel on! You'll embarrass Alison. Have you got any pain-in-the-neck brothers, love?'

'No, there's only me,' said Alison. 'I'm the only child.'

I just knew it. I would have adored being somebody's only child. The centre of everything, with a pile of presents every Christmas and birthday, and a bedroom all to myself with a canopied four-poster bed and an *en suite*.

'Have some sauce,' I said sourly.

Our awful barbecue went on and on. Valjoy came home with Blonk, Spider, Ace and Titch. Alison Ashley looked at them expressionlessly, but tucked her clean little sandals under the garden bench. She still held the sausage daintily in one hand but she'd hardly eaten any of it.

Spider and Blonk revved up an argument about motorbike rally tickets and three dollars' missing change. Mum raised her voice over theirs and told them to shut up and stop that punching and bad language and nick off to their own house if they had one, which she doubted. They wouldn't do either, so Lennie grabbed

Spider by the collar of his leather jacket, and Blonk by the seat of his jeans, and lugged them round to the front and dumped them over the fence.

'It's not fair!' cried Valjoy. 'I'm never allowed to bring my friends home!'

'Don't give me that!' Mum yelled back. 'This place is always neck deep in creepy-looking tech kids who've been suspended from school.'

Valjoy could never stand her friends being criticized, so another battle started and hamburger buns were thrown. Alison's expression didn't change one bit. After a while she got up and said she'd better get home before dark. She thanked Mum politely for asking her to stay for dinner and said she'd had a very nice time – the liar.

She said goodbye to Jedda, Harley, Lennie, Ace, Titch, and even Valjoy, who was sulking by herself under the clothes-line because Mum had won the fight. Mum had a louder and bossier voice than Valjoy.

'You're a real nice well-behaved kid, Alison,' Mum said. 'You come round any time you like and play with Erk. I'm glad she's found you for a girlfriend at school. She doesn't get along very well with the other kids as a rule. Erk, where are your manners? Get up off your numberplate and show your girlfriend to the gate and say tata nicely.'

∾

Jenny Wagner

JOHN BROWN, ROSE AND THE MIDNIGHT CAT

ILLUSTRATED BY RON BROOKS

ROSE'S husband died a long time ago. Now she lived with her dog. His name was John Brown.

John Brown loved Rose, and he looked after her in every way. In summer he sat under the pear tree with her. In winter he watched as she dozed by the fire. All year round he kept her company.

'We are all right, John Brown,' said Rose. 'Just the two of us, you and me.'

One night Rose looked out of the window and saw something move in the garden.

'What's that in the garden, John Brown?' she said. John Brown would not look.

'Out there,' said Rose. 'I think it's a cat.'

'I don't see any cat,' said John Brown.

'I'm sure it's a cat. Go and give it some milk.'

'There's nobody there,' said John Brown.

But that night, when Rose was safe in bed, John Brown went outside. He drew a line around the house and told the midnight cat to stay away. 'We don't need you, cat,' he said. 'We are all right, Rose and I.'

The next night Rose saw the midnight cat as he slipped through the shadow of the pear tree. 'Look, there he is, John Brown,' she said. 'Don't you see him now?'

But John Brown shut his eyes.

Rose sighed and packed up her knitting. Then she wound up the clock and took the milk bottles out. John Brown followed her.

'I'm sure there's no cat,' he said.

But Rose saw the midnight cat often after that. Every night, when John Brown was not looking, she put out a bowl of milk. And every night, when Rose was not looking, John Brown tipped it out again.

'You don't need a cat,' he said. 'You've got me.'

One night the midnight cat jumped up at the window and rubbed his back against the glass. His eyes were like lamps, and his fur shone against the ragged sky.

'Look, John Brown!' said Rose. 'Isn't he beautiful? Get up and let him in.'

'No!' said John Brown, and pulled the curtains shut. 'No, I won't let him in.'

Next morning Rose did not get up. John Brown waited in the kitchen for his breakfast, and nothing happened. He went to see what was wrong.

'I'm sick,' said Rose. 'I'm staying in bed.'

'All day?' said John Brown. 'All day and for ever,' said Rose.

John Brown thought. He thought all through lunch time and when supper time came, he was still thinking.

An hour past supper time he went back to Rose, and woke her gently. 'Will the midnight cat make you better?' he asked.

'Oh yes!' said Rose. 'That's just what I want.'

John Brown went out to the kitchen and opened the door, and the midnight cat came in.

Then Rose got up and sat by the fire, for a while. And the midnight cat sat on the arm of the chair ... and purred.

Christobel Mattingley

NO GUN FOR ASMIR

PHOTO ILLUSTRATION BY DAVID NELSON

BLACK AND WHITE ILLUSTRATIONS BY ELIZABETH HONEY

Asmir and his family make a desperate attempt to catch the last plane out of war-torn Sarajevo — leaving behind his beloved father Muris.

WHEN the bus stopped at last it was outside a big hangar at the airport. There was gunfire from behind and more gunfire from beyond the fence. Asmir looked for their plane. There were several standing on the tarmac. He wondered which one it would be.

He thought they would all get off the bus and hurry inside the hangar to wait. But the driver refused to open the door. He was talking on his little handset. 'The plane's not here yet. So you have to stay aboard until it arrives,' he told his passengers.

Asmir felt the ripple of fear that ran through all the women. And he felt the fidget of impatience growing into a fever in the frustrated and bored children. Everyone was wedged into the seats

like biscuits in a tin. The aisle was piled with bags and boxes. The overhead racks were heavy with rugs and roped-up bundles. There was not a sliver of space to stretch or walk. It was scarcely possible even to wriggle. And the driver would not let them open the windows more than the narrowest crack. So the air became stale and smelly.

Women began to weep as the time dragged on and no plane appeared. Children grew more and more restless and began to cry. 'Please let the children out to relieve themselves,' Asmir's mother asked the driver. 'Just beside the bus,' she pleaded.

At first he refused. But she begged and begged, until at last he gave in. Asmir stood on the step and peed, breathing the outside air that smelled of smoke and burning oil.

Family by family the mothers clambered over the luggage in the aisle to take their children to the door. It was especially hard for the ladies with big baby bellies. Asmir was glad that his mother wasn't like that any more. It was hard enough for her with Eldar in her arms, whining and fretful. She fanned him with her hanky and Asmir played with him to try to stop him crying.

Hour after hour they sat. Pins and needles in the feet gave way to cramp in the legs. Numbness in the bottom became numbness in the heart, and hope turned into sharp icicles of fear. Even the ears became dulled to the sound of mortar bombs, distant and not so far away. And the eyes grew weary with straining for a glimpse of the plane that was supposed to save them.

Asmir produced his two rolls and Mirsada shared them round. But they were tough now and dry, hard to swallow without a drink. Asmir was past being hungry but he gnawed on his crust for something to do. A thick sock of heavy grey cloud had hidden the sun and the afternoon was shrinking steadily. Then suddenly above the sounds of fighting Asmir heard a sound that could have been a plane.

He listened hard and rubbed the fogged-up window with his fist, longing to see the silhouette of their plane on the horizon. He eased the window open another crack. The sound grew louder. It couldn't be mistaken now. It was a plane. A green and grey and brown plane coming in to land.

He nudged Grandmother. She smiled at him. But suddenly Asmir couldn't smile back. This was the plane that was taking them away from Muris.

In a moment they were hurried from the bus and herded into the hangar. It was like a giant's cave, high and hollow and so cold that Asmir's teeth began to chatter. They huddled together for so long that Asmir thought they had been forgotten. Then suddenly they were pushed outside again on to the tarmac in a jostling mob towards the plane.

There was a man in uniform standing at the foot of the gangway leading up to the dark doorway into the plane. 'We'll only take forty,' he said. 'We can't take all of you. Too many kids altogether.'

A moan and a wail went up from the tense tired mothers. Asmir had never heard a sound quite like it. And he never wanted to hear it again. Children began to scream.

Mirsada stepped forward. She spoke in her calm quiet way which made people pause and listen.

'Of course you have regulations. And normally they must be

observed. But this is not normal. And you would not be overloading to take more than forty passengers. After all most of them are children, even babies. And it's not as if we have heaps of excess luggage. We've only got what we could carry. There wouldn't be more than one case each. And the children have only got their little carry bags of treasures. Please take us all,' she pleaded. 'Please.'

The man in uniform looked at her and Asmir was proud of her. She was so beautiful with her long dark hair and her big dark eyes. He looked at Eldar in her arms, and Grandmother who had moved up beside her daughter. Grandmother so frail that she wouldn't have weighed as much as some of the bigger children. It was hard to believe how Grandmother had carried Eldar in her arms, leading all the way on that desperate run for their lives only this morning. So frail but so determined.

Then the man looked at Asmir with his jeans torn at the knees, his scuffed shoes; Asmir trying hard not to cry. Suddenly he seemed to see that their hearts were as raw and blistered as their hands.

'All right,' he said gruffly. 'All aboard. And hurry up. We don't want to hang around here. It's not healthy.'

His mother's smile made Asmir think of the lamp with the pink silk shade at home and how it glowed when it was switched on. 'Thank you,' she said to the man, and Asmir and Grandmother said it too. Eldar gave a proper smile for the first time that day.

'God go with you,' the man muttered. Asmir shook his hand, as he had seen Muris do.

Other families were already scrambling aboard, passing up babies and bundles. By the time Asmir and Mirsada and

Grandmother got inside with Eldar and their luggage, all the seats were taken and they had to sit on the floor.

Asmir had never been in a plane before. He looked around. It was dim and crowded. Through a small window he could see the glow of burning buildings in the distance and the flare of tracer bullets in the dark which had come down like a cloak.

The engines started up and the plane vibrated and throbbed. Children screamed again. Mother soothed Eldar and Grandmother patted Asmir's hand. He knew she was smiling at him in the dark. It was strange how you could be so glad and so sad at the same time. And so scared. If only Muris were with them. Muris had flown many times. If only Muris could be here for Asmir's first flight.

Shuddering into action, the plane lumbered along the runway. There was a thump and Asmir knew they were airborne at last. Climbing, climbing. The fires of Sarajevo disappearing into the distance in the south west. Sarajevo. Home. Muris. Oh Muris! Asmir clenched his raw and aching hands. Come soon, Muris! Asmir had never felt so cold before in all his life. Cold cold cold.

Dorothy Wall

BLINKY BILL

COLOUR ILLUSTRATIONS BY LOUI SILVESTRO
BLACK AND WHITE ILLUSTRATIONS BY THE AUTHOR

*Blinky Bill is bored and bold and mischievous.
And he's off to find adventure . . .*

BLINKY grew into a strong bear. Always up to some mischief, he kept the older bears in a constant state of watchfulness. He was very venturesome and scrambled up to the highest twig on the tree, or out to the farthest branch, scrapping and hugging his playmate or grabbing a nice tender leaf from him just as it was about to pop into Snubby's mouth.

One night Mrs Koala and Mrs Grunty decided to go for a walk. They gathered their cubs together and in a stern voice Mrs Koala gave her orders.

'I'm going for a walk over the hill, Blinky, and don't you move out of this tree. No skylarking and romping while I'm away; and be good to Snubby.'

'Yes, mother,' said Blinky demurely, 'I'll mind Snubby till you come back.'

So Mrs Koala and Mrs Grunty climbed down the tree and, after ambling along the ground in a comical way, they disappeared over the rise of the hill.

Blinky had been watching their progress and he also had heard Mrs Grunty telling his mother about the store on the road where the motor cars went past, and he had a great longing to see these things.

'Stuck in a tree all the time!' he grunted. 'I'm for adventure, snakes or no snakes. I'm not afraid.'

'What are you saying?' inquired Snubby in a tone of wonder.

'I'm going to see those motor cars and the store,' said Blinky in a bold voice.

'Oh! you can't,' said Snubby, quite frightened at the idea. 'Our mothers will be very angry, and besides you'll get lost!'

'I'm going!' said naughty Blinky in a bold voice, 'and you may come too if you like.'

'No! I couldn't,' said Snubby in a terrified whisper. 'Mrs Snake might chase us.'

'If we don't poke faces at her, she won't,' said Blinky. 'I'm going.'

'*Please* don't go, Blinky,' implored Snubby.

'Cry-baby,' mocked Blinky. 'Just show me which way the road lies.'

'Over there,' said little Snubby, pointing his paw to the direction.

'I'll be back in no time; and while I'm away, don't fall out of the tree.' And Blinky started down the tree with a very brave look in his eye.

At the foot of the tree some of the braveness left him. Everything was so strange and the world seemed so large. Even the bushes appeared to look like big trees, and he fancied he could see all kinds of strange faces looking at him round the corners and through the grass. A cricket popped up, just at his feet. Blinky stood still with fright, his heart going pit-a-pat at a great rate.

'Good evening young bear, and where do you think you're going?' the cricket inquired.

'To see the motor cars and the store,' Blinky replied in a very subdued tone.

'Great hoppers!' said the cricket. 'A very bold lad, that's what I think you are.'

'A fellow can't stay at home all the time,' replied Blinky.

'Well, take care you don't come to harm!' And the cricket hopped on its way.

'Cheek,' muttered Blinky to himself. 'Why can't a bear go and see motor cars?'

On he went, sometimes stopping to nibble at a plant that looked extra sweet. It was a great adventure to taste something new and see and smell the bush flowers. After travelling many miles he began to feel tired, so looked around for a gum-tree where a little bear could have a nap in safety.

Finding just the kind he wanted, up he climbed, and there, in a cosy fork between two large branches, he cuddled up and went to sleep, his head snuggled down on his tummy, and his two

front paws folded over his ears. He looked just like a ball of fur, but to anyone trying to spy him in that tree – well, it was impossible. Towards daylight he opened his eyes, and was a little surprised to find himself in a strange land. He had to think quite hard for a time to find out where he really was, then remembering he was on an adventure, he snatched a few leaves and gobbled them up in a great haste, for he wanted to travel before the sun rose too high in the sky. Very carefully he climbed down the tree, as a slip would mean a broken leg or arm, and Mr Blinky knew how to use those strong claws of his. He spread them out in a masterful way, not losing his grip with one leg until he was sure of the other. Once on the ground, he gambolled along just like a toy bear on being wound up with a key.

As the sun climbed higher in the sky he found the tall trees growing thinner, farther apart, and more open ground, also the bush tracks branched off into other tracks. It was puzzling to know which to take, but he kept in mind the direction Snubby had pointed. Another rest during the midday and he felt that his

journey must be nearing its end. He could now hear strange noises, and smell the dust.

'I must be near the motor cars and store,' he thought as slowly he crawled up a tree to see what was in view.

There just ahead of him was the road, and that surely must be the store.

'What a funny place,' thought Blinky.

Down he came, out of the tree, and toddled to the edge of

the bush. There he lay in the scrub, waiting to see all the wonders of the outside world. The sun was setting and something came rushing along the road with two bright lights twinkling. Astonished, Blinky gazed at it. Bu-r-r-r and it was gone, leaving behind a cloud of red dust that nearly blinded him.

'If that's a motor car, I'm sorry I came,' said Blinky slowly, as he brushed the dust from his nose.

Peeping through the bushes again he saw lights in the store and some strange being moving about inside. Waiting until all was quiet, he walked across the roadway. Here was adventure indeed, and just the smallest quake of fear ran through him. Glancing over his shoulder he looked to see how far the bush lay behind, in case he needed to run back at any moment, and then walked right on to the veranda. Over the door were large letters that looked like this:

MISS PIMM

REFRESHMENTS

Puzzled, he gazed at everything, never once thinking of his home that lay many miles behind him. He poked his little nose round the doorway. No one was about, and what a lovely lot of new things to see. Rows and rows of strange things in tins and jars. Bottles on a shelf filled with pretty colours. Some marked 'Raspberry' and others 'Orange'. And good gracious! there were some gum-tips in a bottle standing on the counter.

'I must eat those,' said Blinky to himself, 'they look very juicy.'

Softly he scrambled on to a box, and then another climb, and he stood on the counter.

Looking round all the time to see that no one came unawares, he tiptoed to the gum-tips. From his position behind the bottle he could see Miss Pimm moving about in her kitchen, and judging by the smells that reached his nose she was cooking her dinner. He ate and ate and ate those gum-tips. Such a wonderful 'tuck-in' he had. His tummy grew very round until at last he found he could see Miss Pimm very clearly, as only a few stalks stuck out of the neck of the bottle. They looked very strange standing there, without a leaf to show, and a fat little bear gazing through them

all the while. Next to him stood some big jars of sweets. All labelled in the same strange writing: 'Boiled Lollies', 'Ginger', 'Chocolates', 'Caramels', 'Peppermints'.

'They look nice,' thought Blinky, as he touched the jar with his paws. 'P-e-p-p-e-r-m-i-n-t-s. Perhaps they are really gumleaves,' he thought, and very quietly lifted the lid. His claws were handy for more things than climbing gum-trees.

He scooped a pawful out of the jar, and cautiously tasted one. Finding it hot and very like some plants he had tasted in the bush, he ate more. He went on eating Miss Pimm's peppermints and put in his paw to gather more from the jar. Just as he did so, the lid on which he had been standing slipped from under him, and down it rolled with a terrible thump and bang.

Miss Pimm came running through the house.

'What a smell of eucalyptus! I must have upset a bottle,' she cried to someone in the kitchen.

Blinky got a dreadful fright. He was too frightened to move and just sat there and blinked, one paw in the peppermint jar and the other in his mouth.

'Oh, you robber!' shrieked Miss Pimm, as she caught sight of him. 'Stealing my peppermints. I'll teach you – you young cub,' and she grasped a ruler that lay on the shelf.

'It's life or death,' thought Blinky very quickly, and made a dart off the counter and round the corner, right into a large tin of biscuits. Fortunately the tin was nearly empty, so there was plenty of room to hide.

'You young scallawag,' cried Miss Pimm, 'wait until I catch you. All my gum-tips gone as well.' This seemed to put new vigour into her actions and she fairly flew round the shop. To Blinky, hiding away in the biscuit tin she sounded more like an elephant rushing round than anything else. Round the corner she came and then, catching sight of Blinky in the tin, she banged the lid down with an awful crash.

'I've got you now, you young thief,' she called out triumphantly. 'You won't get out of there in a hurry, and to make sure of you, I'll get a box to put you in.'

Blinky was breathless. Whatever was going to happen? Would he be killed or taken to one of those zoos that Mrs Grunty spoke about? I must get out of here, he thought, and waste no time about it.

Listening with his ear to the side of the tin, he heard Miss Pimm's footsteps going towards the kitchen, then pushing open the lid a little way with his head he peeped out. Everything was safe. She was still away, but he could hear her talking and rummaging about outside. Quickly he climbed out of the tin and was walking round the back of the counter looking for a place to hide when he heard Miss Pimm's footsteps coming back again.

'Oh dear, what shall I do?' he panted. 'She'll catch me for sure this time.' He dived into a sack of potatoes just as she came through the doorway.

'You'll stay in this box now, young man,' said Miss Pimm, 'and I'll sell you to the first person who wants a young thief.' She tramped round to the biscuit tin. Imagine her rage when she found the tin open and no bear there.

'He's the devil himself,' she cried, and started to open every tin she could find. Next she looked round the boxes of fruit, and under the counter, then sniffing loudly, she came to the sack of potatoes.

'So you'd make all my potatoes taste of eucalyptus. Well, we'll see about that. Where's my box?'

She rushed over to the door to get the box, and at the same moment Blinky jumped out of the sack of potatoes. But she saw him. Round the counter she came, the box under her arm, and round the other way rushed Blinky.

'Stop! Stop! I tell you,' she screamed. But Blinky had no idea of stopping. He popped in and out of corners, over tins, under bags, and Miss Pimm after him. It was a terrible scuttle and the whole shop seemed to shake. Bottles and tins rattled on the shelves, the door banged, papers flew everywhere, and in the middle of all the din Miss Pimm tripped over a broom that was standing against the counter. Down she fell, box and all. The clatter was dreadful and her cries were worse. Blinky was terrified. How he wished a gum-tree would spring up through the floor. Suddenly, all in a twinkling, he saw a big bin standing open beside him and without any thought of what might be inside, he climbed up the side and

flopped in. It was half full of oatmeal. Using both paws as quickly as he could, he scratched a hole in the oatmeal, wriggled and wriggled down as far as he could until he was quite hidden: all that could be seen was a little black nose breathing very quickly. He kept his eyes closed very tightly, and felt very uncomfortable all over: but he was safe at last.

Miss Pimm slowly picked herself up. Her side was hurt and her leg was bruised. The box was broken and also the broom handle. She seemed quite dazed and felt her head. Then, holding on to the counter with one hand she limped round the back of it once more.

'You'll die this time, when I get you,' and she seemed to choke the words out.

Every tin, every sack, and every box was moved and examined, but no bear was to be found. She didn't stop to have her tea, but went on searching, hour after hour, and all the store had to be tidied up again. After a very long time she locked the door leading on to the roadway, and Blinky, feeling the benefit of his rest and becoming bolder each minute, peeped over the top of the oatmeal bin. He saw Miss Pimm taking a little packet from a case marked 'A.S.P.R.O.'. He popped down again as he felt quite safe in the bin, but he listened with his large ears to any sound she made.

Presently the lights went out, and after mumbling to herself about the 'young cub', she went through to the kitchen. Blinky could see the moon shining through the window-panes and he very, very quietly and gently crawled out of the bin. A shower of oatmeal flew over the floor as he landed on his feet and shook his coat and ears, so that oatmeal was everywhere. Right on to the window-ledge he climbed, trod all over the apples in the window that Miss Pimm had so carefully polished, and sat down for a few minutes on a box of chocolates, then noticing more peppermints in the window he pushed a pawful into his mouth and munched away in great content. The window was open half way up so he climbed up the side and sat on the open sill, feeling very brave and happy. What a tale he would have to tell Snubby when he reached home.

'Click!' The light in the store was on.

Blinky wasted no more time on thoughts. He was off that window-ledge and across the road in a few seconds. He reached the edge of the bush safely and turned round to see what was happening. Miss Pimm stood in front of the store with a big policeman, pointing to the open window, and then they looked across the roadway to the bush where Blinky lay hidden behind a tree.

'Well, it's a pity he got away,' Blinky heard the policeman say, 'as the Zoo would have paid you well to have had that young bear. I didn't know there were any about here; and I've lived in the district for thirty years.'

'I'd have given him gladly to the Zoo and no payment in return,' said Miss Pimm savagely, 'if they had offered to replace the peppermints and oatmeal.'

The next day when some motorists stopped at Miss Pimm's

store and bought some biscuits, they wondered why the biscuits had such a strong taste of eucalyptus.

Blinky now felt a 'man of the world'; but he thought it wise to go home before any more adventures came his way. So walking along and running sometimes as fast as his funny little legs would take him, he came to the tall tree where he had rested the night before.

Climbing up to the same branch he was asleep in no time and slept all through the night until the birds woke him at dawn, with their chattering. Two kookaburras flew into the tree where he lay and laughed very loudly as they saw Blinky curled up in the corner.

'I'll tell Jacko, if you laugh at me,' he said, in a loud voice. 'He's my godfather.'

'We were only laughing at the white stuff on your nose,' the kookaburras explained. 'It looks so funny.' Blinky rubbed his nose with his paw, and found it still covered with oatmeal, then grunting angrily he stood up and gave himself a shake. 'I must be going,' he said. And down the tree he climbed and on to the ground again.

He wondered if he had been away from home very long, and began to feel a little uncomfortable about his greeting when he did arrive. Would mother be very angry? Perhaps she was still away with Mrs Grunty. But his fears did not last very long, as a bee flew across his pathway, and he became very curious about that bee. It flew to a flower to gather the pollen. Blinky trotted along to see what it was doing and watched very closely as the bee buzzed about dipping its small head into the heart of the flower. Something warned him not to touch it; but being a little boy bear, he just couldn't watch any longer without giving a poke. So out came his paw, and he reached to pat it. He tried to play with it; but the bee objected, and with a loud buzz stung him right on the nose. Oh, how he cried, and danced about, rubbing his nose with his paws. He ran on blindly, not looking to see where he was going, and after some minutes, when the pain stopped, he found he had lost his way. He had taken a wrong turning on the bush track, and now – what would happen?

Blinky sat down to think things over. While he was puzzling his brain, and wondering which way to turn, a kind little green lizard peeped through the grass and said in a very small voice:

'What's the matter, Blinky? You look very sorry for yourself!'

'I'm lost,' replied Blinky, 'and I don't know how to find my way home.'

'I know where you live,' said the lizard joyfully. 'You follow me, and I'll lead the way.'

'I'm so glad I met you,' Blinky replied. And, as the lizard walked ahead, he followed, never taking his eyes off her. In and out of the grass and under bushes she ran at an amazing speed, until they reached the path again.

'You're safe now,' she said, turning to Blinky, 'keep straight ahead and your gum-tree is not far away.'

'Thank you, Miss Lizard,' said Blinky politely. 'I must hurry as my mother is waiting for me.'

On he ran. It seemed a long way to him, and how he wished Angelina would hop along and take him on her back.

As he came to the top of the hill, he saw his home down in

the hollow, and he was quite sure he could hear his mother calling for him.

Hurrying along, faster than ever, he now heard grunts and cries, and his heart went pit-a-pat as though it would jump out of his skin.

Suddenly his mother saw him. She grunted loudly with joy, and Mrs Grunty and Snubby joined in the chorus.

'I'm here, mother,' Blinky called. 'I'm at the foot of the tree.'

'Oh, you naughty cub. Where have you been? Just wait until you climb up the tree – '

'Don't smack me, mother,' Blinky whimpered. 'I'll never run away again.'

Bit by bit he climbed the tree, all the time imploring his mother not to spank him. He was so long in reaching the branch where Mrs Koala and Mrs Grunty and Snubby were waiting, and they were so pleased to see him safely home, that Mrs Koala forgot to spank him. She hugged him and petted him and Snubby laughed and danced on the branch. It was good to be home, but Blinky still wondered if his mother would remember to punish him. But she didn't. She did not forget. Mothers don't do those things, but she wanted Blinky to think she did.

'Where have you been all this time?' she inquired.

'I saw Miss Pimm and a big policeman,' Blinky said in a loud voice. 'And I ate Miss Pimm's peppermints.'

'Wonder it did not kill the young lubber,' said Mrs Grunty.

Snubby's eyes nearly fell out of his head as he listened to Blinky's story, when later on in the evening they sat together in the fork of the tree whispering and giggling as Blinky told him all about his adventures. When at last he cuddled up and went to sleep, close to his mother, Mrs Koala could be seen rubbing a gumleaf over a very swollen little nose.

Doug MacLeod

THE HUMAN FLY FROM BENDIGO

ILLUSTRATED BY PETER THOMSON

MY favourite uncle, Tim McFife,
Was very keen on circus life.
He had an act which stole the show –
'The Human Fly from Bendigo'.

Each night, he showed his expertise
And balanced on the high trapeze
Then, spreading both his silver wings,
He fluttered round the Roman rings.

As spotlights blazed on Uncle Tim,
A thousand eyes were fixed on him,
A phantom flying to and fro –
'The Human Fly from Bendigo'.

And so he stunned them every night,
Dressed up in foil and party lights,
Suspended by a handy wire
To keep him flying ever higher.

One dreadful night, the wire went slack
And Uncle landed on his back
But, ever faithful to his pride,
He kicked his legs, buzzed once, then died.

Caroline Macdonald

THROUGH THE WITCH'S WINDOW

COLOUR ILLUSTRATION BY MARK SOFILAS

BLACK AND WHITE ILLUSTRATIONS BY MARK WILSON

When Rose Tattoo wheels another barrow-load of junk out of the tip,
four children and an enormous yellow dog follow her.

THE children watched the woman with the wheelbarrow. There was nothing else to do, really. At first it had been fun exploring the tip and watching Peter's dog Chainsaw chase rats through the stinkier parts.

But the local council put up notices saying KEEP OUT and NO SCAVENGING. An ogre from the council was sitting in a hut inside the gates all the time, and the only people allowed in were those driving trucks or cars with trailers of rubbish to fill up the tip.

Except for *her*. The children saw her push her wheelbarrow straight *past* the savage guardian in his hut – the ogre who'd shouted at them and threatened to have Chainsaw put down.

The woman walked right past the ogre, and he didn't even look up from his newspaper. It was as if he hadn't seen her. It was as if she knew how to make herself *invisible*.

It was the same when she came out of the tip again. The ogre ignored her and her barrow full of junk. Chainsaw growled wildly when she walked past the children as they stood outside the caravan park, watching.

'Let's follow her,' said Erana. She was the oldest, but only by a month and two days.

'It's nearly time for tea,' said Stu, her younger brother.

'Can't be,' said Peter, who was from the caravan next to Erana and Stu's. 'It's not dark yet.' He could see their four parents sitting around a card table between the two caravans and he could tell by their concentration on the game that tea wouldn't be ready for ages. 'Okay. Let's follow her.'

Yvonne, Peter's little sister, didn't say anything. She was looking at her new fifth-birthday socks with the sparkling embroidered flowers and butterflies around their tops, and she was

thinking that the day after your birthday is the saddest day of the whole year.

When the woman with the wheelbarrow disappeared around the bend in the road, the children stood up and ran after her.

Peter kept a firm hold on Chainsaw's collar, because he knew Chainsaw was fascinated by the woman's clumping gumboots and her billowing overalls. Peter knew that what Chainsaw thought was a game could seem like an attack to some people. He'd worried for a long time after the tip-ogre's threat to have Chainsaw put down, just because Chainsaw had flown at his rustling newspaper.

The road was empty around the corner. She'd disappeared. 'Not even a puff of smoke,' Erana whispered.

'She can't have disappeared,' said Stu.

They walked on cautiously. The sides of the road were dark with dense black pine trees. Soon they were walking very slowly.

Yvonne was trailing after them, wishing they could go home now. Night time seemed to be coming very quickly. There were cracking noises in the trees all around them, and Yvonne knew that Chainsaw couldn't protect them if monsters leapt out from all directions. She broke into a run to catch up and banged into Erana, who'd stopped and was pointing at something beside the road.

It looked like a large black cat perched on a pole, ears flattened, ready to spring at them. The children tensed, waiting, but Chainsaw wasn't alarmed. He ran over and lifted his leg against the pole.

'It's not real,' Erana said. 'It's a letterbox, I think, made of old tin or something.' She touched it, feeling the roundness of its shape, a definite head.

'It looks like a wombat! Isn't that weird? And I can just read the name on it. *Rose Tattoo*.'

'Rose Tattoo,' Peter echoed. 'That must be *her*.'

Then they saw a glimmer of light through the gloom of the pine trees. The children crept closer. A glow from the house shone dimly on the brown wheelbarrow. It stood at the bottom of three

steps leading up to a tiny verandah and a wooden door. On both sides of the door were high windows like two slit eyes.

The children watched Rose Tattoo's house for a while, keeping themselves hidden among the pines. Sometimes a light showed in one window, sometimes in the other.

'We'd better go home,' said Peter, who was getting tired of keeping Chainsaw still and quiet. 'It's nearly dark.'

Erana found the moving light behind the windows almost hypnotic. The windows were like two eyes winking, one open for a few seconds, and then the other. 'Let's have a look in,' she said.

Again they crept forward, this time until they stood beside the wheelbarrow.

Yvonne was hanging on to Chainsaw's tail.

The windows were too high. Peter pushed Chainsaw towards

Erana. 'Hold on to his collar,' he said. 'Yvonne, you're the littlest. Climb on my back and have a look.' He crouched and put his hands behind his back to make a ledge for her feet, and she scrambled up. He straightened his knees, and her head became level with the windowsill.

Yvonne peeped into the room. Almost immediately she screamed loudly and leapt off Peter's back. She was sobbing, and her eyes were wide with fright.

Peter grabbed her hand and the children ran into hiding among the pine trees. Yvonne was squeezing words out between sobs.

'Her face was just – just floating there! She had this big shiny sword thing and she cut this boy's head off! She was holding his head and – and – and it was all dripping with blood! And she was laughing!'

'Aw, Yvonne,' Stu said, but his voice didn't sound as scornful as he'd wanted it to, and he and the other two looked back at the house uneasily. Yvonne had her arms around Chainsaw's neck, crying into the fur at his scruff.

Then they saw it: Rose Tattoo's face looming at the window, lips stretched back, her teeth shining in the light from the fiery sword beside her.

They didn't discuss it. They just ran – to the road, around the corner, back to the caravan park.

∽

Margaret Barbalet

THE WOLF

ILLUSTRATED BY JANE TANNER

THE first time Tal heard the wolf he didn't believe it. He went back to sleep. The next time it woke all of them. But after a while they fell asleep again.

Next morning in the kitchen, however, things were not the same. Around the breakfast table they began to discuss wolves.

'They don't live *here*, in this country,' their mother said firmly.

'Where *do* they live?' Dai, the youngest, asked.

Tal and Megan looked at each other. Mother didn't answer. Then it was time to go to school and they forgot about Dai's question.

That night Tal heard the wolf in their own garden.

Next morning before their mother was even awake, Tal got out the encyclopaedia.

'We live in open peaceful country. We always have.' Megan was close to tears. 'They can't come here.'

Together they looked at the coloured pictures. There was a wolf eating a bloodied mess, red leaking into the snow. Tal shut the book. They knew Dai must never see it.

That night Tal was unable to go to sleep.

He thought of the hill that sheltered their house, the trees and rocks they had always played amongst. They knew every tree and every rock. They always walked to school. Their friends came over to play. As he went to sleep Tal thought, *I think of it always as sunlit, peaceful. I know it rains, but I think of it as a peaceful place.*

He awoke to Dai's scream, to the house shaking as their mother ran downstairs to lock the windows.

The howling went on and on. He knew it was the wolf coming closer. It was worse than he could have imagined. It was worse than his nightmares.

It was the worst thing, coming closer every night.

The next day, without even mentioning wolves, their mother outlined some of the new rules.

They would have to always play inside. The doors would have to be bolted and barred. Here mother looked at Tal. He was sometimes careless.

'What about school?' Dai asked.

Their mother frowned. 'I'll have to take you in the car.'

'Every day?' Megan asked, then stopped. 'Of course it'll be every day. I wasn't thinking.'

That night their mother went around the house bolting shut all the windows. Some of them had never been bolted before, and stuck. She had to force and wedge them shut. It took a long time and it was dark by the time she had finished.

'I'm covered in lumps,' announced Dai at breakfast. He pulled up his pyjama jacket. His chest and tummy looked like an archipelago.

'They weren't there yesterday,' mother decided. 'Let's see if they go by tomorrow.'

She packed the bag to take out to the car. In the new routine they all followed her and jumped in as she slammed shut the front door.

I just wish she'd say something, anything . . . Tal thought as they drove off to school. She didn't talk about the wolf; she had just changed everything.

Next day Dai's lumps had grown together from islands to continents.

'It might be something he ate,' mother pretended, rubbing in the cream they used for mosquito bites.

It might be the wolf, Tal thought silently, *just the idea of it*.

That night Tal awoke aware that Dai had been crying for some time. Megan stood helplessly by his bed. Mother came downstairs from her bedroom.

'What's the matter? Have you had a dream?'

'No, I'm crying because the wolf's come. Because it used to be safe and now it's not.'

Tal heard his mother kiss Dai and tuck him in her own bed. Later he heard crying again.

In secret at school Tal read all about families who had lived surrounded by wolves. He looked at the snow and tundra where the wolves prowled. At home their garden was turning into a wilderness.

At night now they ate dinner trying to talk of other things, to argue the way they had before the wolf came. Mother often turned on the radio so that there would be a cheerful background noise. After a few weeks Tal noticed that she always hummed the same tune, a new one that went down and down.

In bed he would hear the howling coming closer and closer, leaping over the garden wall. Then he would hear the wolf prowling around the house, testing every doorknob, pressing every window latch. Some nights he lay rigid with fear so that he had to turn on his bedside light. He would fall asleep with it on.

In the kitchen one weekend when Megan and Dai were watching television, he asked about his cat.

'What if I left it out?'

His mother turned, horrified, her hands covered in flour.

'I mean, would that satisfy the wolf? Would it go away?'

'Oh, love,' she said hugging him. 'Of course it wouldn't.'

'What if I went out?' he said beginning to cry. 'It would be worth it for Megan and Dai. Dai's little.'

She hugged him again. 'Tal, I know what you mean. But you can't make it go away.'

'Can anyone?'

'No.'

Megan had been the loudest girl he had ever known. Now she was so busy that she didn't have time to shout.

'I want to make it like before the wolf came. I think about that every day,' she said brushing her teeth that night.

'But you can't,' Tal said kindly.

'Well, I will,' she shouted and rushed into her own room.

Later through the wall he heard her beginning to hum. It was the same final tune that his mother always sang.

Months passed. They stopped talking about the wolf. It came every night and they were no longer shocked. Tal had his birthday and asked a few friends. He played his records very loud and after they had all left he realised that no one had even mentioned the wolf.

'You know, I don't think it's as loud as it used to be any more,' he said. 'And from the front this just looks like a normal house.'

His mother looked at him startled, then interested.

That night he sat in his room surrounded by all his new presents (more than usual, he guessed, to make up for the wolf).

He thought of the time before the wolf came, and saw it as distant, green and sunlit, his family in a dream that he could never go back to. It was like being younger, he thought; that too was dear to him. And yet he couldn't ever have it back again. In the flames of the candles on his cake he had seen himself, unable to go back ever to the last year.

A week after his birthday when they were washing up his mother said out of a long silence, 'You know, I think you're right. It's definitely a lot softer than it used to be.'

'But still close,' he began. 'You know, Mum, there's a boy at school whose family lived surrounded by wolves for a whole year!'

'What did they do?'

'The same as us. Boarded up their windows, stayed inside all the time.'

'And now?'

'It was a different country, Mum, not *here.*'

Tal noticed next that while the wolf still prowled around every night it often whined and growled instead of howling. Once Tal went to the window at night in the silences between its howls. He could hear it outside, scratching and panting. He imagined its tongue bobbing on an open jaw among the row of teeth. He put his face up to the boards one night but all he could see was a crack of night sky.

Half a year passed. Megan had her birthday.

Dai adapted to life inside; inventing new games for them all on the stairs. Tal supposed they might never go outside in the garden again.

Then towards the end of the year, his mother put down her papers as he came in to say goodnight. It was something from work as usual.

'I'd like you not to tell the others this, Tal, but I've seen the wolf. I took down a board from a high up window.'

As Tal stared she said, 'He's not as big as I thought.'

A week later Tal had a dream. A voice came out of the night: he couldn't tell from where. And the voice spoke and said one thing over and over again: *Let it in, let it in.* Only when he woke up did he realise that the voice was his own.

Tal crept downstairs before it was light to bake Mum's cake on the morning of her birthday. He always did this. When the cake was in the oven he made himself some breakfast.

Suddenly he heard a rasping. Something was snoring right outside the kitchen door. Suddenly he had to see.

He went and found a strong kitchen knife and levered off one end of a board. It cracked as he took it away. Sunlight flooded his face; as startling as the sight of the wolf, awakened by the sound, bounding away in fright over their garden wall.

When his mother saw the missing board she smiled. Tal was so relieved that he found himself telling her about his dream and the voice saying, *Let it in, let it in.*

'I've had the same dream lately,' she said.

That night he had the dream again. He awoke in the dark still

hearing the voice. In his pyjamas he went down the stairs. He could hear the wolf outside the door, whining. Suddenly he realised that it was almost morning, half light. He wanted more than anything to go outside.

Let it in, let it in, said the voice at his elbow.

With a reckless movement he took down the bar, cobwebbed and dirty, and opened the lock on the door. Then he pulled open the door, wide, and stood back.

There stood the wolf, dirty and thin. Its hair was matted and grey. It looked at him and then limped past into the living room and lay down in front of the dying fire's warmth. It left muddy footprints and its tail knocked down a magazine.

Outside the garden waited, green and wonderful, just touched with the colour of sunrise.

Tal went and woke the others and led them, holding Dai's hand, down to the living room.

'I've let the wolf in,' he said proudly. He smiled. 'I think it might become our dog.'

Colin Thiele

STORM-BOY

ILLUSTRATED BY ROBERT INGPEN

*When Storm-Boy finds three orphaned pelicans he brings them to the
rough little humpy where he lives with his father.*

BEFORE long the three pelicans were big and strong.
Their white necks curved up cleanly, their creels grew,
and their upper beaks shone like pink pearl-shell. Every
morning they spread their great white wings with the bold black
edges and flew three or four times round the humpy and the beach
near by to make sure that everything was in order for the new
day. By then they thought it was time for breakfast, so they landed
heavily beside the humpy, took a few dignified steps forward, and
lined up at the back door. If Hide-Away and Storm-Boy were still
in bed, the three birds stood politely for a little while waiting for
some sign of movement or greeting. But if nothing happened Mr
Proud and Mr Ponder began to get impatient after five or ten
minutes and started rattling their beaks in disapproval – a snippery-
snappery, snickery-snackery sort of sound like dry reeds
crackling – until someone woke up.

'All right! All right!' Storm-Boy would say sleepily. 'I can hear you, Mr Proud!'

He would sit up and look at the three gentlemen standing there on parade.

'I know what you're thinking, Mr Ponder. Time for respectable people to be up.'

'Time for respectable pelicans to get their *own* breakfast,' Hide-Away grumbled, 'instead of begging from their friends.'

And as time went on, he really meant what he said.

At last Hide-Away spoke sternly to Storm-Boy.

'Mr Proud, Mr Ponder, and Mr Percival will have to go back to the sanctuary where they came from. We just can't afford to feed them any more.'

Storm-Boy was sad but he always knew when his father had made up his mind. 'Yes, Dad,' he said.

'We'll put them in the big fish-baskets,' said Hide-Away, 'and take them in the boat.'

'Yes, Dad,' said Storm-Boy, hanging his head.

So they caught Mr Proud first, and then Mr Ponder, held their wings against their sides, and put them firmly in the fish-baskets. Neither Mr Proud nor Mr Ponder thought much of the idea. They snackered noisily at Hide-Away, raked their ruffled feathers crossly, and glared out through the wickerwork with their yellow eyes.

'Huh!' Hide-Away laughed. 'We've offended the two gentlemen. Never mind, it's all for their own good,' and he bowed first to Mr Proud and then to Mr Ponder.

But when it came to Mr Percival's turn, Storm-Boy couldn't bear to see him shut up too. Ever since the miracle of Mr Percival's rescue, he had been Storm-Boy's favourite. He was always quieter, more gentle, and more trusting than his two brothers. Storm-Boy picked him up, smoothed his wings, and held him close. 'Poor Mr Percival,' he said gently. He looked up at his father. 'I'll hold Mr Percival,' he said. 'Can I, Dad?'

'Oh, all right,' Hide-Away said, taking up the two baskets. 'Come on, it's time we started.'

Hide-Away sailed for five miles up the sanctuary before he stopped the boat.

'Here we are,' he said at last.

Then he opened the two baskets and took out Mr Proud and Mr Ponder.

'Off you go,' he said. 'Now you'll have to look after yourselves.' Then he pushed them off. They flew away in a high wide arc and made for the shore.

'Now Mr Percival,' he said.

Storm-Boy pressed his head against Mr Percival's and gave his friend a last soft squeeze. 'Good-bye, Mr Percival,' he said. He had to pause for a second to clear his throat. 'Be a . . . be a good pelican, Mr Percival, and look after yourself.'

He lifted him over the side of the boat and put him down on the water as if he were a big rubber duck. Mr Percival looked surprised and pained for a minute and floated up and down on the ripples. Then he lifted his big wings, pedalled strongly, and rose slowly up over the water.

Storm-Boy brushed at his eye with his knuckles and looked away. He didn't want to let his father see his face.

Hide-Away and Storm-Boy spent the day fishing. It was fine and sunny, but somehow it seemed cold. Most of the time they just sat in the bobbing boat without talking, but Storm-Boy knew that his father knew what he was thinking. Sometimes Hide-Away looked at him strangely, and once he even cleared his throat carefully, gazed out across the water, and said in an unhappy gay voice: 'Well, I wonder how the three Mr P's are feeling. As happy as Larry, I'll bet!' He looked rather miserably at Storm-Boy and went on with his fishing.

'Yes, I'll bet,' Storm-Boy said, and also went on sadly with his fishing.

Towards evening they packed up and set off for home.

The sun was flinging a million golden mirrors in a lane across the water. It glowed on the bare patches of the sandhills and lit up the bushes and tussocks till every stem and twig shone with rosy fire. The little boat came gliding in to shore through the chuckle of the ripples.

Suddenly Storm-Boy looked up.

'Look, Dad! Look!' he shouted.

Hide-Away beached the boat and looked up to where Storm-Boy was pointing. 'What?'

'Look! Look!' cried Storm-Boy.

High against the sky on the big sandhill stood the tall Look-Out Post that Hide-Away and Fingerbone had put up years before. And right on top of the post was a big shape. It was quite still, a statue on a column, a bird of stone.

Then, as if hearing Storm-Boy's startled voice, it suddenly spread out two big wings and launched itself into the air. As it banked against the western sun its beak and big black-tipped wings glowed in the shooting beams of light. For an instant it looked like a magic bird. Storm-Boy ran ahead, craning upwards, yelling and waving.

'Mr Percival! It's Mr Percival! Mr Percival has come back home!'

It was a happy reunion that night. Even Hide-Away seemed secretly glad that Mr Percival had come back.

'Yes, I suppose he can stay,' he said; 'as long as Mr Proud and Mr Ponder don't come back too. One pelican's appetite is bad enough; we can't cope with three.'

And although Storm-Boy loved Mr Proud and Mr Ponder too, he found himself hoping very much that they would stay away.

And they did. As the days went by they sometimes swept overhead, or even landed on the beach for a while, but in the end they always returned to the sanctuary.

But not Mr Percival. He refused even to leave Storm-Boy's side.

Nan Chauncy

TANGARA

COLOUR ILLUSTRATION BY DAVID LEGGE
BLACK AND WHITE ILLUSTRATIONS BY BETINA OGDEN

*Through the old shell necklace Lexi meets Merrina, the Aboriginal girl,
whose tribe — the last surviving in Tasmania — live hidden
in 'Blacks' Gully'.*

BREAKFAST was late, waiting for Andy. There had been
some bother over sheep and he went to Wanderon to
ring the Boss. When he hurried in, he said, 'Whew! Hot!
This weather's like Christmas, not like spring. Must be thunder
about. Well, Snowy! Aren't you lucky to have had it so fine? And,
look — not a cloud in the sky for your last day.'

'My — last — day?'

She turned slowly from the window, where she had been
watching the firetail finches playing round the yellow broom, and
stared at him. Andy couldn't mean she must go home tomorrow?
He couldn't — ! What about Merrina?

'Don't look like that, my pet,' Beth said as she brought in eggs
sizzling on the hot dish. 'You'll be coming again before long —

won't she, Andy? And there's all today – and tomorrow morning, too, I suppose.'

'Yes,' joked Andy, 'plenty of time to make life a misery for a poor old dog, dragging him for a walk.'

'Oh, Andy, is there? Tomorrow, too?' she asked, with an eagerness that could seem unkind to a dumb animal, though of course Uncle Podger was far, very far from being dumb.

'Sit down,' said Beth, 'and tell us what the Boss said, Andy. He didn't stay long in Melbourne?'

Lexie only half-heard the talk about Daddy's plans, and Kent already returning to school, and the furniture and luggage Mrs Callan and Mrs Sterk were bringing from their old home to store in one of the empty rooms at Wanderon.

'So Lexie will have lessons like a big girl, and be able to read all the books she wants soon,' said Beth, 'and the house comfy and nice meals made by Mrs Sterk – you like her, don't you, Lexie?'

'Yes, Terkie's nice,' she answered absently. Could it be that Merrina would wait and wait at Cleft Rock, wait for a Weetah who never came ...? But there was today, and tomorrow, too, for walks with Uncle Podger. Time beyond that was years and years away.

Andy had been right about the heat; it was very muggy in the glade under the tree-fern umbrellas; even in the open bit before the rock the air was close and still.

Lexie peeped round suspiciously: nothing moved, not so much as a tree-creeper prodding under bark for insects, but then Merrina had tricked her so many times before.

A horrible little thought wriggled in her mind like the mosquito wrigglers in the tank – today Merrina would not come. The mothers might want her – anything! Indeed, how did she ever know when Lexie arrived?

To drive the thought away, she stumped about not caring if she made twice as much noise as an old rowitta, and sang haltingly, without any confidence:

O the young emu, and the little kangaroo,
The little joey and the bandicoot . . .

She paused and listened to the silence listening to her. Her throat felt dry: she tried not to mind the silence and to go on singing about the white bush rat, when – thud! – a small stone landed in a bare patch in front of her right shoe.

'O the young emu, Weetah!' mocked Merrina, capering out on the little ledge before the cleft. 'Oh wah! . . . wah! . . . wah!' and she stamped her feet nimbly.

'Where were you? I couldn't see you, Merrina. How did you know I was here?'

The fun and laughter left Merrina's face: she sprang lightly to the ferns and came to Lexie. Squatting before her on the ground she patted her shoe and looked steadfastly at her face as she said softly, 'I'll always know when you want me, Weetah – always.'

The way she said it made Lexie want to cry. After a little pause she blurted out, 'I've got to go home soon. You won't come and play with me then, Merrina?'

'You must come here.'

The tears welled and spilled over: Lexie put her hands over her face and sank down on a moss-covered rock. When she went home she knew Blacks' Gully would be as far away as the moon from the earth. 'I won't be let,' she sobbed.

Merrina's arms folded on her knees and her head bent over them: her shoulders shook. When she lifted her short black curls and looked up, her face was as wet as Lexie's. She said again, miserably, 'I'll always know when you want me, Weetah.'

But they couldn't crouch in the ferns for ever, breaking their hearts over something that hadn't yet happened. Overhead on a branch an olive thickhead watched them and mocked at their tears with his call, 'I'll *wet* you! . . . I'll *wet* you!'

Merrina's arm reached out from where she crouched, seized and flung the small stone and nearly hit him. She was all smiles again as she bounded to her feet, scooped up a handful of pebbles and threw one after another at the perch he left quivering, till she hit it. It was very thin.

'You try, Weetah!'

Lexie shook her head: the mark was much too small and far off. It was quite hopeless, she couldn't even hit the tree itself. Merrina was shocked. 'Baby Trewella, my little brother, could do better than that. Try again.'

She tried and tried: Merrina was merciless, first one hand then the other, till Lexie felt they would drop off. She rebelled, 'I can't any more, my arms are too tired.'

Merrina still looked anxious. 'You must throw all the time, every day, throw at anything that moves. Or what will happen,

Weetah? How will you kill things when you are big? How will you get birds for the hungry fathers?'

Her distress was so great, Lexie had one last try and by some fluke managed to hit the tree. Merrina could not applaud – no, that was not possible, but she showed approval by treating Lexie as a stone, picking her up in her strong, thin arms and pretending to throw her at the mark. They both toppled over in the ferns and scrapped like two puppies.

Merrina sprang up shouting, 'Tangara! . . . Tangara!'

'Tangara!' echoed Lexie happily, for she had learned the word, a favourite of Merrina's, and knew it meant 'Let's set off again, let's go to another place!'

Merrina was already leaping to the cleft in the rock.

A new tangara! Lexie was excited: they were following the ledge she had always longed to explore. A ledge was queer, you could only go along it forwards or back: on one side was a steep high wall, on the other a deep, dark place stuffed with trees. Sometimes the ledge was so narrow you wished the wall had knobs to be clutched, sometimes wide and choked with great rocks that had to be climbed or squeezed round.

Tangara this time led – Lexie remembered the path – to the great half-circle of smooth stone under the cliffs, the place of many little fires with the mothers watching them, and the children playing. She called to Merrina in front, 'Will *they* be there?'

'No, not the fathers, Weetah.'

The surprising ledge here broadened out to hold a long, shallow pool filled with rainwater. The rock behind was slimy and dripped and oozed: it had wet pockets and small, dry caves in it.

After chasing a frog, and quenching her thirst, Merrina strutted to one such pocket and rummaged inside.

Over her shoulder she said, 'Merrina and Weetah will appear in beauty before the mothers,' and showed packets made of wide bluegum leaves, pinned together with splinters of wood.

Lexie thought she meant 'wash face and hands', and did so, using her hanky as a towel. Merrina thought this only half-doing things: she herself rolled in the pool swooshing most of the water out, then danced on the warm rock to dry herself.

'Yes, well, I'm going to paddle,' Lexie cried, not to be outdone. She sat in a dry spot and removed her shoes, then quickly peeled off the fawn socks which were the colour of her sunburned legs.

Merrina had forgotten about the zipper fastening: she gave a yelp of horror to see her friend stripping the skin from her feet, then laughed till tears came. 'Nar!' she ordered, 'that you must do for the mothers, Weetah!'

When Lexie had her shoes on again, she combed her hair with her fingers and thought she was ready, but Merrina was still titivating. She was using a small, round pot-hole of brown water as a looking-glass, rubbing grease on her curls and sprinkling her hair with a red powder from a gum-leaf bag, and squatting down close to admire herself the better.

A few pale everlasting flowers bloomed in a crevice of the wall above: she ran to fetch them, twining them in her hair with as much care as a society lady arranging her diamond tiara for a ball. 'Merrina looks beautiful!' she beamed at the grinning face in the water; snatching another packet, she added a powdering of fine charcoal to her skin, with a few streaks of red also, on her face.

For a few moments she capered round admiring herself with the greatest satisfaction: then she remembered her poor friend with the shameful white skin – what could be done for her? Full of kindliness she advanced on Lexie with the charcoal bag: 'For you, Weetah!'

Lexie dodged back and the bag ripped apart, spilling the powder. Merrina gave a frightened glance round, then she giggled. They scooped up what they could and put everything away in the rocky holes.

Lexie washed her hands again, smoothed her yellow dress which was also rather black, and followed Merrina once more along the ledge.

They came to a place of wonders, columns of stone like tree trunks through which they threaded a way. The ledge seemed to have vanished into the gully and Lexie guessed they were at the beginning of the cliffs, about to step into the open space. Her feet grew heavy, she held back timidly. 'Wait, Merrina!'

Merrina turned with a reassuring smile: in her hand was a small sapling she had rooted up. 'Hold this in your hand, Weetah, and walk first.'

'Look, Merrina, I'm afraid Uncle Podger ... I ought to go.' But she could only go forwards or back, and now Merrina was behind with a loving hand pressed on her shoulder.

'They won't hurt you, Weetah.'

'No, I know that, but ...'

'Don't you want to see my little brother, Trewella?'

'Yes, but ...'

Merrina gave a firm push. Having no choice, Lexie stepped from the place of columns to the wide half-moon of space, a leafy sapling quivering in her hand as a sign that she came in peace.

Max Fatchen

A Short, Summery Thin, Thong Song

ILLUSTRATED BY MICHAEL ATCHISON

THE song
of a
thong
is a
flip,
flap,
flong
that echoes
wherever
you go.

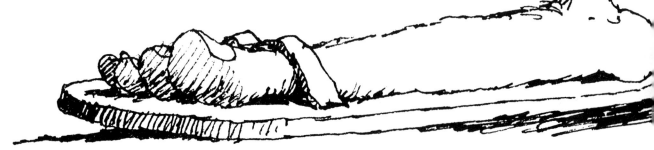

There aren't
any places
for silly
old laces
but a thing
that holds
on to
your toe.

You're flapping
and tapping
with feet
overlapping
and people who watch
will agree
that the song
of a thong
when you're
flopping along
is of feet
that are born
to be
free.

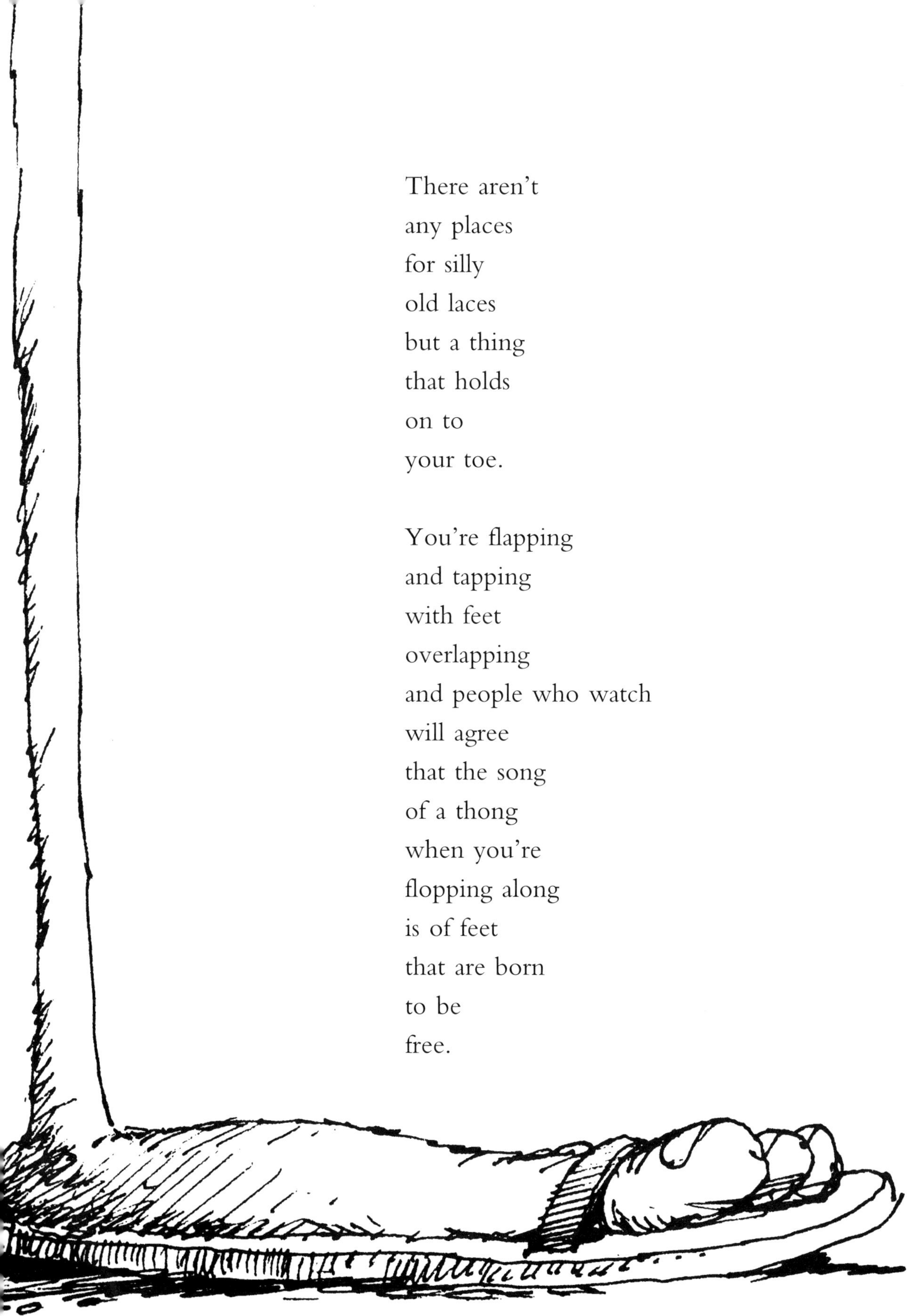

Victor Kelleher

WHERE THE WHALES SING

ILLUSTRATED BY VIVIENNE GOODMAN

In a wild storm at sea, Claire sees her father washed overboard.
Alone, hungry and terrified, how will she survive?

CHINKS of sunlight showed at the edges of the hatch; and the only sounds were the creaking of the boat and the slosh of water across the floor. Foolishly, she swung herself straight out of the bunk, causing the pain in her knee and thigh to return with a rush. Again she almost blacked out and had to cling onto the bunk to prevent herself from falling.

When her vision and her breathing steadied, she groped her way to the ladder, opened the hatch, and dragged herself up into the sunlight. Although the sea was still running high, the wind had dropped and the sky was a clear, uniform blue. As the boat drifted up

210

onto one of the crests, she swept her eyes around the horizon, hoping for a sight of land or a glimpse of some passing vessel. But the white-capped sea was empty; and over to the west there was not even a smudge of grey to mark the Australian coastline.

She nearly started to cry again then and had to press her hands to her eyes to stop any tears escaping. They'll be looking for me by now, she told herself silently. In planes and boats and everything. They'll be sure to find me by nightfall.

She went on repeating that message to herself throughout the day. Sometimes she muttered the words aloud, to ward off loneliness and to keep her mind off the dull pain in her leg. For a while she believed so completely in what she was saying that she did not budge from the cockpit in case she missed some passing boat or plane. By mid afternoon, however, she was less sure; and she took time off to go below for a drink and to collect a tin of food from the emergency supplies.

The sea, meanwhile, had grown calmer, and for that reason much emptier. Back in the cockpit, eating beans from the tin, she was less eager to scan the horizon. There seemed little point. Also, she felt too hot to go on searching – far hotter than the spring sunshine warranted.

I must be sickening for something, she thought vaguely, and she peeled off her life-jacket and parka, stripping down to the lightweight wet-suit she wore beneath.

She had meant only to toss her discarded clothes onto the nearby seat, but somehow they slid over the stern and into the sea. Not that she really cared. The feverish heat in her body told her she would not need them again. Neither did she need any more to eat. She threw the tin aside and that also slipped over the stern.

As it sank through the sunlit depths, something moved towards it: a long sleek form that butted the strange object with its nose before spiralling upwards. A glistening grey arc broke the surface, like a perfect miniature of the great whale body she had glimpsed beneath the boat during the storm. And abruptly a whole school of dolphins was playing around the boat. Leaping and diving, they cut zigzag paths across each other's wakes, leaving behind a thin tracery of bubbles that glittered and shone.

Somewhere in the coolness of the waning day, she could hear someone laughing; and she guessed it was herself, glad not to be alone any longer.

Then, just as suddenly as the dolphins had arrived, they were gone, and it was late evening, merging into night. Habit told her she should go below, lie down on the bunk and sleep. And she truly believed that was what she had done – until she woke from a dream in the middle of the night and discovered she was still lying in the open, her body bathed in sweat.

In the dream she had been swimming amongst the dolphins, their round eyes watching her curiously as she dived with them down into the blue depths, the sea cool and soothing on her bare skin. By contrast, the night felt hot and sticky, the watchful stars much less friendly than her animal companions. So she quickly closed her eyes and willed herself back into the dream, leaving the loneliness and discomfort of the waking world far behind.

She was not sure when she next woke. The painful throbbing in her leg returned and she sat up and looked out across a sea as flat and smooth as a lake. The sun was high, beating down mercilessly, the atmosphere stiflingly hot, as was she. There was no sign of the dolphins. The only movement was in the sea immediately around the boat, where she could detect the constant swirls and eddies of an ocean current that was bearing her towards the south. But why there? she wondered hazily.

For no reason that she could explain, she recalled how the humpback whale had risen beneath her, as though using its great body to buffet the boat off course, away from the land. It had been replaced by its dolphin cousins, their much smaller bodies swimming easily in and out of her dreams. She shook her head in confusion. Had they also been directing her, she asked herself, and should she follow?

Just asking the question was enough. It wasn't like being at home, with parents advising her or ordering her about. Here, there was only the windless day, the air grown furnace-hot, clinging to her skin like flame. And in response to the unbearable heat, she leaned out over the side.

Within arm's reach the sea glittered enticingly, as if urging her on; but as a precaution she took a short coil of rope from beneath the cockpit, tied one end to a stern-post, and flung the other end into the sea. Before she followed it, she paused briefly, amazed at her own audacity. Then she was plunging straight down into the placid blue of another world, exactly as in the dream. And as in the dream, all the unbearable heat left her body. Even the pain in her leg dissolved away, leaving her free to twist and turn as she pleased.

High above, she could see the rope, a thin white tentacle trailing behind the boat. The sight of it aroused an earlier fear, of being left behind, abandoned, and she shot hastily to the surface. But to her relief she found that the current was bearing her along too; she and the boat drifting southwards together.

She ceased to worry after that. Like the boat, she gave herself to the ocean, satisfied by its silky cool touch. For what seemed to be hours, she swam lazily to and fro or dived deep; sinking down to where the sunlight barely reached and she was surrounded by soft darkness, her ears filled with the sound of her own heartbeat.

It was during one of these dives that she first became aware of an icy chill welling up from the depths. She shivered and stared into the formless gloom. At the limits of her vision she could see something moving: a large shadowy body swimming as lazily as

she. Yet watchful, and drawing always nearer.

She recognised instantly what it was. The sleek head, the jutting dorsal fin, could have belonged to only one creature. A shark! Again she was caught in an upsurge of icy water that made her whole body shake with cold, and she turned in panic and arrowed up towards the boat hovering there in the calm blue of the day.

Always, during previous dives, the boat had remained floating above her, as if waiting. Yet now, while she was still struggling to reach the surface, it began drifting away, drawn on by the warm current, leaving her in the clutches of this much colder water that had lured the shark from the depths.

With silver bubbles billowing from her mouth, she kicked out desperately, fearful that at any moment the toothed mouth would snatch at her legs. The surface rushed to meet her and she burst free. Out into an ocean much wider and emptier than she remembered. A desolate blue waste in which she was no more than a tiny speck. Frantically, she swung around, searching. The boat was already out of reach, but the end of the rope was still swishing past, and she lunged and caught it with both hands.

As she was tugged along, half-buried in a smother of foam, she glimpsed the shark from the corner of her eye, its dorsal fin cutting the water over to her right. Purposely, she jack-knifed her body, driving herself under; and through a froth of bubbles and sun-streaked water, she saw the streamlined body swimming parallel to her own. Idly flicking its tail, it veered in towards her, one expressionless eye observing her coldly as it slid beneath her exposed belly and half-turned.

'No!' she screamed out, not to the air and sky, but to the vast watery spaces of the ocean. 'Get away!'

Her cries seemed to go no further than herself; to be swallowed up by the blue-black emptiness. And again the shark was sliding beneath her, its rough sandpaper skin rasping against her legs as it passed. Shuddering from the contact, she surfaced long enough to gulp in air and then jack-knifed down once more, convinced that if she took her eyes off the creature for more than a few seconds it would strike.

The rope was biting into her palms now, her arms and shoulders aching from the effort of holding on. There was also the cold to contend with, her limbs growing stiff and unresponsive. So that when the shark angled in for the third time, she could not kick out in self-defence, even though it slowed as it brushed against her: its body as icy cold as the surrounding water; its tail slapping her aside with cruel playfulness.

'Help me,' she murmured softly, as if pleading with the ocean itself. 'Please make it go away.'

The only response, more heartless even than the silence, was the appearance of another dark shape swimming up from the deep. It was bigger than the shark – longer, far bulkier – and moving with strangely ponderous speed.

This new danger was more than she could bear. Choked with terror, she clawed at the rope, lost her grip entirely, and surfaced in a flurry of foam.

Immediately the shark closed in, its dorsal fin cutting a straight, deadly line through the water. But before it could reach her, something glittered and broke far beneath them – a succession of bubbles that exploded from the dark shape swimming below and spun upwards. The bubbles reached the surface in long thin lines, like strings of silvery beads; a curtain of them that formed a protective circle around her helpless body.

Although that enclosing circle was made of nothing but air, the shark was unwilling to enter it. As it halted its rush and slanted away, several smaller shapes followed the ascending bubbles. Their tails pumping energetically, they drove at the shark, scaring it off; their beak-like mouths issuing excited, clicking cries as they leaped gracefully from the water.

Claire felt one of the bodies rise gently beneath her, its skin unexpectedly warm, reassuring. Just as gently, it bore her across the surface towards the boat and floated there while she reached up with trembling hands and gripped the side.

Only when she was safely on board did she fully realise what had happened. And by then the dolphins, their job done, had disappeared. The bulky shape far below had also gone, back into the darkness from which it had come. Though she knew it now for what it was: not a shark at all, but a great whale, the air from its lungs forming the net of bubbles that had saved her.

Perhaps because she had read about those glittering circles of bubbles, she was not surprised. 'Thank you,' she whispered through chattering teeth. And with her chilled body pressed against the hot planking, she drifted back into unconsciousness.

∾

Anthony Hill

THE BURNT STICK

ILLUSTRATED BY MARK SOFILAS

John Jagamarra was happy at Dryborough Station in the red inland
country where he lived with his mother and his people.
Yet nothing goes on forever . . .

ONE night, when the young moon had risen and they were sitting around the fire, Charlie Warragin, the head stockman, looked at John's mother and said, 'Liyan, I have heard they are coming to take away your son in the morning.'

John Jagamarra felt his mother become very tense, her fear flowing into himself. She held him tighter in her arms and cried, 'Who is coming to take him away? Where will they take him?'

'The Big Man from Welfare,' said Charlie Warragin. 'I have heard he is travelling with the police truck to all the camps in this part of the country, and taking the light-skinned ones to the Fathers at Pearl Bay. He was with the mob at Richmond Downs the day before yesterday. He will be here tomorrow.'

'When will they bring my son back to me?'

'He will not be coming back,' said Charlie Warragin. And the old man, Jabal, who knew much and taught the law to the young men, agreed. 'They will bring him up in the ways of the white man. It will be many years before he can return, but his life will never be the same.'

'They cannot do this thing!' cried Liyan.

'They can, and they will. It is the law of the white man that says so.'

'I will tell the Boss . . . tell Mrs Grainger. She will stop them.'

'She will be able to do nothing.'

'I love my son! This is his family! They cannot come to take him away!'

'They have been coming from the day he was born,' said Jabal.

John Jagamarra heard his mother begin to weep, and he cried with her though he did not fully understand. She picked him up, and held him close to her breast, and rocked him as she had when he was a baby. She wept with a low wordless sound, and he felt the tears wet on his naked skin.

'I will run with him into the desert country and we will hide from the Big Man.'

'There is nowhere safe to run,' said Charlie Warragin, 'and in the end they will find him.'

When he finished speaking, John's grandmother and all the other women in the camp began to moan and cry with grief, as they did when one of the people died and their spirits returned to the Ancestors. They beat the ground, and threw dust over themselves, and mourned for the loss of one of their own.

The grieving went on late into the night. The fire had burnt to ashes and the young moon had almost finished his journey across the sky before the camp lay down to sleep. But Liyan did not rest that night. Her son slept against her breast, yet she sat awake through the hours wondering what she could do to stop the Big Man from taking John and sending him to the Fathers at Pearl Bay Mission.

And then an idea came to her.

Very early, when the first splinter of light appeared in the eastern sky and before the dawn birds had started singing, Liyan woke her boy. 'Come,' she said, 'there is something we can do.'

They went to the campfire where the cinders were cold. Liyan took a stick that had burnt black almost to charcoal. She ground the soot and the charred ends of the stick into a powder in the

palm of her hand, and began to rub it into John Jagamarra's skin.

She rubbed it into his feet and up his legs and all along his back. She rubbed it over his belly and chest. She rubbed it into his hands and along his arms. She rubbed it on his neck, and over his face, and into the strands of his brown hair. So that when the rest of the camp woke up that morning, John Jagamarra had been changed. His light-brown skin was now dark as the others – and how they laughed when they saw him, and said what a clever thing Liyan had done.

'I would not have thought of that,' remarked the old man, Jabal.

But Charlie Warragin asked, 'Will it be enough to trick the Big Man from Welfare?'

'Oh yes,' said John Jagamarra's grandmother. 'Even I might not have known him unless I looked closely – and as for the white men, we all look much the same to them.'

That morning, when the sun had risen, the men and the older children left the camp: some to the stockyards, some into the back country where they could not be asked questions. Only the women and youngest children were left at the camp under the acacia trees. And there they were, sitting silently, when the Big Man drove in the truck down the track from the station homestead. There were two policemen as well, and the Boss's wife, Mrs Grainger, sitting between them.

The truck had a kind of wire cage on the back, with a gate that padlocked and canvas blinds that rolled down if the sun got too hot, or if they didn't want you to see if anyone were locked inside.

They got out and stood uncomfortably on the other side of the campfire. The two policemen and Harriet Grainger did not like what they were about to do. But it was the law.

'Which one is Liyan?' asked the Big Man from Welfare. He was a tall man, as his name implied, with freckles and sandy hair and pale blue watercoloured eyes, squinting in the morning sun.

'I bin Liyan, boss,' said John Jagamarra's mother softly, in the shy Pidgin talk with which her people mocked the white man's speech.

'I am told you have a son,' said the Big Man, 'who must come with me to Pearl Bay.'

'Why, boss?'

'Because he must be taught the white man's way . . . to read and write in English, to count and to learn a trade. The blackfeller's way is not enough for him. You know that. It is the same for all those with the light-coloured skins.'

'But my boy does not have a light-coloured skin, boss.'

'I have been told differently.'

The Big Man from Welfare was beginning to sound impatient and the sun was hurting his eyes. 'Isn't that so, Mrs Grainger?' He looked to the Boss's wife, standing there twisting her wedding ring and wishing she were anywhere else instead.

'Oh, Liyan,' said Harriet Grainger. 'I'm sorry. It's not right. But there was nothing I could do.'

'That's okay, missus,' said Liyan. 'We're all blackfellers in this mob. Isn't that so? Do you want to see, boss?'

John Jagamarra stood up next to his mother, the sun behind him. His skin, where Liyan had rubbed it with the burnt stick was the colour of earth when the shadow falls upon it. But she was careful not to touch him as she ached to do, in case the charcoal brushed away, showing the light-brown flesh underneath.

Nobody said a thing. Even Mrs Grainger was silent as the Big Man walked across to the boy and his mother, and stood looking down at them. The sun shining directly into his water-rinsed eyes, for the women had placed themselves carefully. He looked from one to the other for a very long time.

'Is this your son?' he asked at last.

'Yes, boss,' answered Liyan.

'Is it?' He turned angrily to Mrs Grainger.

'That is John Jagamarra,' the woman replied uneasily.

'Then there has been a mistake. I have been wasting my time.' And without speaking another word, the Big Man from Welfare and the two policemen who were with him, got into the truck and drove away.

There was much laughter and clapping of hands in the camp when they had gone. The women ran up to Liyan and John Jagamarra, and hugged them. They said what a cunning trick it was that had been played on the Big Man, and how proud the men would be when they heard of its success. The children ran down to the waterhole to swim and to wash away the charcoal from John Jagamarra's body.

Only Mrs Grainger, who had stayed behind, seemed doubtful. 'It *was* a clever thing to do,' she said, 'and it shows how much you love your son. But Liyan, was it wise? Don't you think the men from Government will hear of it and come back one day?'

'Who's going to tell them, missus? Not us.'

'Nor I,' said Harriet Grainger. 'But they have their books and their papers and ways of finding things out. And if that happens, won't it be worse for you and your boy?'

'Ah,' replied Liyan, 'do not worry yourself, missus. If the Big Man comes back, I will use the burnt stick once again.'

'It may not work a second time,' said Harriet Grainger.

Eleanor Nilsson

THE BLACK DUCK

ILLUSTRATIONS BY BETINA OGDEN

When Tom's family left their farm, they also left behind Squeak Toy,
the wild black duck that was Tom's special pet.

TWO months passed. The ash trees in Tom's street turned to red then burgundy and the air grew cooler in the evenings. Tom played every day with David and sometimes with David's friend Russell as well. His mother often watched him from the window as it came his turn to ride on David's trike.

One day David let him ride it home and keep it overnight. Tom's mother watched him polishing the trike with a tissue, wiping the seat down, shining up the handlebars, even cleaning between the spokes in the wheels. She smiled afterwards when she thought about it, and it gave her an idea.

'Tom,' she said that night. 'It's your birthday next month. Dad and I are going to give you what you want the most. There,' she said, as Tom stared at her, 'we'll say no more about it, but it will be something to look forward to.'

Slowly Tom started to smile, almost a frightened smile at first. His mother had known then, all the time.

She was pleased. She hugged him. 'There, off to bed now, Tom.'

Tom went to his bedroom and looked at all the photos on his chest of drawers. He picked up the one of Squeak Toy no bigger than a sparrow, downy and soft, sitting in one of his hands. He'd been a patient boy. The farm had made him good at waiting. He only had to wait now till his birthday. His mother had already shown him where to start counting off the numbers on his calendar. He took it down and put a big black mark across the day that had just passed.

The next day he tried not to think about it too much. It was still so far away. But at night he carefully scored off another day. And gradually the days peeled away from the calendar and brought him closer to what he wanted the most.

'Aunty Joan's coming for my birthday,' he told David and Russell the day before it. 'She's bringing my presents. Dad'll be at work. It'll just be me and Mum and Aunty Joan and the presents. I'll show you after.'

David smiled.

'Joan,' echoed Russell. 'Your aunty got the shop? Near the oval?'

'No,' said Tom, puzzled. 'I don't think so.'

'Worse luck. We go there lots, don't we, Dave? For liquorice.'

David nodded, his red hair falling over his eyes.

That night Tom couldn't sleep. He kept imagining the sounds that Squeak Toy made and listening for the beat of her wings. He felt tired out when he got up in the morning, heavy-eyed but beaming.

'You're the one should be the butcher,' said his mother, 'with a smile like that. I haven't seen you smile like that since ...' But she stopped herself just in time.

Tom had breakfast, then he rushed out to his chair in the back garden, and smiled over the fence at Mrs Lindberg. She found it even more worrying having him smile steadily at her, instead of just staring with his solemn blue eyes. Then, to fill in the time, he went down to see David, but his house had a shut, empty feel and nobody came to the door.

He walked up to the Blackwood roundabout to wait for Aunty Joan. He could imagine her faded blue car coming up the main Coromandel Valley road, with the cobwebs hanging on to the door and a big box with holes in it inside on the back seat. He felt quite sick, almost as if he were walking upside-down.

Tom stood jigging about beside Aunty Joan's car. There was a big box, beautifully wrapped, on the back seat. Tom peered in, to see where the holes were. Aunty Joan kissed him.

'Run in and tell Mum I'm here,' she said. 'And stay inside while we get your surprise out of the boot.'

Tom opened the gate and ran up the little path. He felt a bit puzzled. His surprise was on the back seat.

'You sit in the lounge, Tom,' said his mother, all smiles, 'and Aunty Joan and I will bring in your present.'

'Presents,' said Tom.

'Oh yes. Presents. Aunty Joan will have something nice for you too.'

Tom shut his eyes till the black that he saw turned red and then black again as he squeezed his eyes tighter and tighter shut. He bounced up and down on the settee, his face breaking into smiles. Then he heard the sound of paper crackling and felt his

mum and Aunty Joan come into the lounge with something big.

'Now,' said his mother.

Tom opened his eyes. There was a beautiful red shiny trike with silver handlebars and a silver bell waiting for him on the cream rug.

He looked from Aunty Joan to his mother and back.

'Aunty Joan's been keeping it for us,' explained his mother, 'so that you wouldn't see it before your birthday. Isn't it a beauty? Now you and David can have such rides together.'

'Yes,' said Tom, but his voice sounded a little flat. He stood up, though, smoothed his hands along the handlebars, tore away the bit of wrapping that was on the trike, and sat on the seat. He could just touch the ground with his feet.

He looked up worriedly at Aunty Joan.

'Oh yes, Tom,' she said. 'My present. I'll just bring it in.'

And she brought in the big box. It was covered in gold and blue striped paper and it had a big gold bow on the top. Tom felt anxious for he couldn't see any holes in the box. Didn't Aunty Joan know?

He took the box and sat down on the settee with it. Then very slowly and carefully he took off the gold bow and the striped wrapping paper, and then, very, very gently he pulled at the top of the carton.

There was no movement inside and the box felt light. He pulled at the flaps and peered into the darkness. But it was a duck, right enough. There was a duck, sitting quietly in the darkness.

'Beep, beep,' whispered Tom, but nothing answered.

'She's too frightened,' he thought.

He looked up with such a smile then put his hands down into the carton, to find and feel the little duck. But it felt wrong. He looked at what his hands were holding. He lifted it out. It was a rubber duck. Aunty Joan had given him a rubber duck!

She was beaming at him placidly. 'Is that all right for you, Tom? Life size, the man said. It's to remind you of that nice little duck you had at the farm, remember? We sat one day and watched it swim. It was like a rubber toy. This one squeaks just the same. Try it, Tom.'

Tom couldn't believe it. He stared at her, then at his mother. Then he threw the toy on to the floor.

'Now, Tom,' said his mother sternly, 'that's no way to behave. Take your trike outside then go to your room.'

Tom, his face hot, marched out, taking his trike with him but kicking its wheel viciously as he went. He wished it were Aunty Joan.

He heard her saying, 'Is it too young for him? I'm sorry, Margaret. I never know what to buy him.'

Patricia Wrightson

THE SUGAR-GUM TREE

ILLUSTRATED BY DAVID COX

Like many best friends Sarah and Penny often had fights.
But the dispute about the tree-house was different.

S ARAH was making a house, under the sugar-gum tree in
her back yard. Penny came round to help. There was a lot
of stuff lying around the tree. Penny had a good look.
'Where did the rug come from?' she asked.

'The tip,' Sarah told her. 'When Dad took me. It's clean, even. Mum helped me.'

'It's magic. What are the bricks for?'

'The stove, I think. Or it could be chairs.'

'There's a lot. You can have a little stove and two chairs.'

Sarah frowned; she hadn't made up her mind. She said, 'The stove has to fit the pan Mum gave me.'

Penny went to look at the pan. 'Cups too!' she cried. 'Your mother gave you cups!'

'Only two,' said Sarah. 'And they're cracked.'

'I was going to bring my old teaset!'

'You still can,' said Sarah quickly, because she could tell that Penny was hurt. 'We need more cups and there's no teapot.'

'You know my teapot's broken,' Penny said in grumpy way. She *was* hurt.

The house was made from an old quilt. Sarah tied it to the tree with string.

'That needs a nail,' said Penny. She was good with nails. She went into Mr Bell's shed, and came back with a hammer and a nail.

'Oh, Penny!' cried Sarah. 'You can't put a nail in Dad's good sugar-gum tree!' Sarah was good with string, and it was her house.

'If a wind comes,' said Penny, 'the whole house could blow away.'

She stood on an apple-crate and nailed the quilt to the tree.

'Now you've made the house crooked,' Sarah told her crossly.

Penny reached up to pull the quilt straight. There was a loud, cracking noise, and she tumbled down. The thin wood of the apple-crate had broken.

'Look what you've done!' cried Sarah. 'That was my table! Penny May, you're a gloop!'

Penny stood up slowly. She was frowning, and there was a long, red scratch on her leg. She said, 'That's not very nice. Calling people a . . .'

'A gloop,' said Sarah, helping in a grown-up way.

'. . . when they've fallen down and hurt their leg and they're only trying to help. You ought to say sorry.'

'Me?' said Sarah, smiling her grown-up smile. '*You* ought to say sorry. Putting nails into Dad's tree and breaking my table. Go on. Say you're sorry.'

Penny shut her lips tight. Her face went red.

She jumped at a branch of the sugar-gum tree, pulled herself up and began to climb.

'Come down!' Sarah called, but Penny went on climbing. 'You're just being another gloop!' cried Sarah.

Penny climbed quite high. Then she sat in the fork of a branch and shouted angrily:

'I won't come down till you say you're sorry!'

Sarah was upset; but of course she wasn't sorry. It was her house, and people should make their house their own way. It wasn't fair for Sarah to say sorry when Penny was the one to

blame. But when would Penny come down from the tree?

Sarah didn't know what to do, so she went on making the house. Penny went on sitting in the tree. She didn't even look down, but stared away over all the back yards.

Sarah put the old rug into the house for a floor. She carried bricks in, and made a stove and two chairs. She turned the apple-crate over to hide the broken part, and put it in the place for a table. She put the cups on the table and the pan on the stove.

Penny was still sitting in the tree.

'I think that looks nice,' said Sarah. She said it to herself but loudly, in case Penny wanted to come down and look. 'But there ought to be flowers.' She went to the geraniums under her bedroom window, and picked some flowers. She put them in a cup on the table.

Penny stared away at the back yards.

'It's nearly dinner-time,' said Sarah, to herself but loudly. 'Dad will be home soon.' She waited for a bit, but nothing happened.

Sarah went slowly to the back door. Maybe her mother could sort things out.

∾

Allan Baillie

LITTLE BROTHER

COLOUR ILLUSTRATION BY JANE TANNER
BLACK AND WHITE ILLUSTRATIONS BY BETINA OGDEN

Cambodia . . . and the Khmer Rouge are in power. Vithy has lost everyone and everything he loved – except his older brother Mang. Now they have been separated.

VITHY walked no more than a hundred metres along a muddy path before he reached a bitumen road. The road – any road – was menacing because it meant trucks full of soldiers at any minute and Vithy wanted to turn back to his safe forest. But he had to find Mang and he had to start by finding out where *he*, Vithy, was.

He stayed behind a tree and tried to work out where the road went. It was a year ago, but he could remember the Khmer Rouge making him, Mum, Sorei, Mang and eighty neighbours march south from Sambor for thirteen days. And the soldiers had then taken Mum, Sorei, him and forty-eight other people across the River Mekong, leaving Mang and the others on the other side . . .

For a moment Vithy's face loosened. Then he pressed his lips

together and shook his head, as if to dislodge a thought.

'Okay,' he told the tree.

Okay so they took Mum, Sorei and him to the Big Paddy. Forget about what happened there. Doesn't matter now. But he didn't know where the Big Paddy was for a start. Mang had joined him months ago, but yesterday soldiers marched them and some others into the forest for many hours – maybe to kill them because there wasn't enough rice – until someone started shelling the forest. They had run blindly from the soldiers in the confusion and he did not know how long they had run, nor in what direction. So he knew only that he was a long way south of Sambor, somewhere in the middle of Kampuchea. And west of the Mekong.

'What can you do with that?' he asked the tree.

He punched the tree, thought a bit and punched the tree again.

'Nothing,' he said finally and started following the road to his right.

At first Vithy walked through the trees beside the road, but there seemed to be nothing on the road at all. It is slow, hard work to push through undergrowth with an open road beside you. And the road had been torn apart by craters and trenches, as if armies had fought with field guns for this strip of old bitumen. This must be why nobody was using the road: no truck could drive on it.

Vithy left the trees for the grass verge, and after less than an hour he was striding down the centre of the road with the confidence of a band on parade.

So he hopped and jumped down a chain of craters on a bend,

and nearly stumbled into a truck.

The truck was painted khaki and heavily loaded. It was stationary. Four men, stripped to the waist, were working with picks and shovels to fill in a crater. A fully uniformed soldier was leaning against the truck, watching.

The officer looked up and saw Vithy. 'Heya,' he called.

Vithy ran very fast, very low into the forest. He tore into shrubs, weaved between trees, jumped a fallen log and hunched for the sound of shots.

But there were no shots at all.

Vithy's jagged race became a jog, then a panting rest. He trembled, swallowed and listened, but nobody was following him. He waited for an hour, and thought about what he had seen.

They wore uniforms.

Not black pyjamas, or pieces of uniforms like the Khmer Rouge he had known, but full brown uniforms from the caps to the boots. They were different. Go back and look.

Vithy closed his eyes and shook his head.

They're just stupid mountain men. That's what Mang said.

No!

In the end he crept slowly back to the road, his heart drumming in his ears. He had to know what they were.

The soldiers were levelling another crater as if nobody had ever seen him. They put their shirts on and the officer drove the truck off slowly. Too late Vithy smelt the bagged rice. He squinted after the truck and slowly worked things out. 'Not the same soldiers,' he said aloud, and walked onto the road to hunt for spilled rice.

A long while ago the Khmer Rouge had come down from the mountains of Cambodia, conquered the country and called it Kampuchea. Now, was it possible that some other army was conquering them? Did these soldiers fire the shells that gave Mang and him the chance to escape?

Vithy found five grains, put them in his mouth and sucked them as he walked on. By mid afternoon the forest had peeled away from the road and was replaced by huge rice paddies with no rice and no people. He heard engines revving on the road ahead and slid quietly through the paddies until the sound was far behind him. Then he returned to the road.

As the sun set he was beginning to pass houses, first singly, then groups and streets. A sign told him he was in the outskirts of

Phnom Penh, the capital of Cambodia, but he could not believe it. He had known the river edge of Phnom Penh in festivals and a family holiday, and it had been a swirl of colour and noise, honking cars and revving motor bikes pushing against a river of people. But in this city everything was deserted.

Vithy walked on as the silence slid coldly up his spine. The buildings grew taller and crowded together as he moved into a darkening stone desert. The only sound he could hear was the nervous slap of his bare feet on the bitumen and the soft whispering of the wind in the streets. He thought of shouting at the city but he decided against it. What if some *thing* howled back?

Vithy stopped at a broad intersection and bit his lip. Now he knew exactly where he was and he wished he didn't. He had come here before the war with Dad, Mum and thousands of people for the music, lights and gaiety. Now there were only empty bandstands and stages in the long park to his right. To his left there were trains, long rows of slowly rusting metal, and beyond that there should have been a cathedral with an elephant grazing by its front door. Now, no elephant, no cathedral, nothing at all.

He walked slowly towards the centre of the city, feeling colder with each step. He passed many cars left by the side of the road, smashed, dented, sometimes burnt. A touch of wind whirled paper out of the gutter. Vithy was watching more paper money than he'd ever seen in his life littering the street. Awnings sagged from buildings with shattered windows and stained walls. Shops were bare and open.

Vithy reached the city's central market, a huge empty concrete dome, and looked for a place to sleep among the looted jewellers, tailors, radio shops. He entered a jeweller's shop through a kicked-in door and used a torn piece of curtain to sweep enough dust off the floor to sleep. He sprawled in the shadows and began to drift away from this city of ghosts . . .

'Eh! Come on. I can see you!'

Vithy jerked to his elbows as a shadow in the street rattled the screen over the window. He pushed himself desperately away from the shadow until he backed into a wall and was showered in glass. A piece of thin metal jabbed his finger and he grabbed it between his thumb and forefinger to defend himself. It was no bigger than a bottle top.

They had caught him. He knew they would.

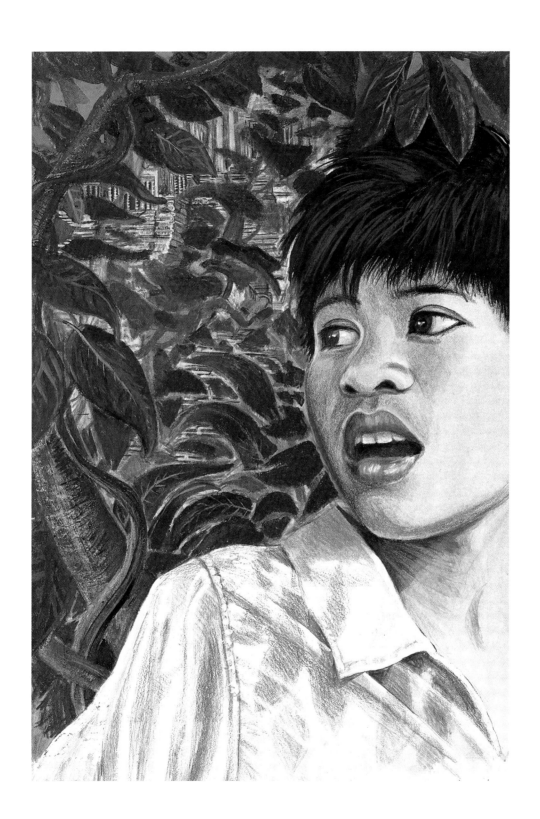

Doug MacLeod

VAMPIRE VISIT

ILLUSTRATED BY PETER THOMSON

A pint of blood is all I need
To get me through the night,
A tiny peck around the neck
Will fill me with delight.

I'm sure you have a pint to spare,
Your veins look fairly ample,
So, save a vampire from despair
And let me have a sample.

Please put away that wooden stake,
It looks a trifle sharp.
Be careful now, for heaven's sake,
You'll stab me through the hea-a-a-a a-a-a-a-rt!

Gillian Rubinstein

THE GIANT'S TOOTH

ILLUSTRATED BY CRAIG SMITH

Are there really giants? Is there really a tooth fairy? What is the white thing Troy and Tania discover on the beach?

TROY and Tania lived near the beach.
Not far from their house a huge rock, shaped like a pillow, rose out of the sand. Troy and Tania called it the Giant's Pillow.

On the first day of the summer holidays, Tania spent the whole morning making a bed in the sand. The sheets were seagrass and the quilt was kelp, and the pillow was the

rock, the Giant's Pillow. The bed had to be enormous to fit the pillow. Troy and Tania lay down on it in the afternoon and watched the gulls strut and squabble on the sand. The sea came hissing almost right up to the bed, and then it turned and went hissing away again. The bed did not get wet.

Then the sandpipers came and it was time to go home for tea.

'I'm going to play that game again tomorrow,' Tania said, as they walked home.

'Stop wiggling your tooth,' Troy told her.

'I can't help it; it's loose.'

No one else came to the beach. It was silvery, windy, lonely.

In the morning Tania ran to the beach first while Troy was still eating his breakfast. The waves were high and noisy, and the sand stung her legs. The big bed looked rumpled as though someone had slept in it, and there were funny squiggles on the sand like writing.

'It's just the wind,' Tania said to herself, wiggling her tooth with her tongue. But there was something behind the rock that had not been there before. It gleamed and flashed in the sun.

Tania walked carefully all round it. It looked like a little, shiny, pearly-white footstool. She touched it. It was as hard as bone. She sat down on it.

When Troy came running up, she shouted, 'Look, Troy, look what the sea washed up – a little chair. And it's mine. I found it.'

'The bed looks just like someone's slept in it,' Troy said. 'And who's been writing on the sand? I suppose it's the wind.' Then he looked carefully at the little white chair. 'It looks just like something . . .' he said. 'But I can't remember what! Get up, Tania, let me sit on it.'

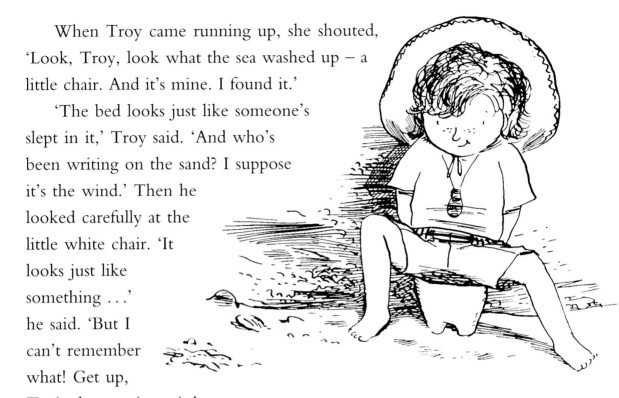

Tania got up, and Troy sat on the chair, and Tania walked all round it again, and then she said quickly, 'I know what it looks just like! It looks just like a tooth!'

Troy jumped off it, and ran to his sister. They stood very close together, and they looked from the Pillow rock to the white thing and back again.

'It is a tooth,' Troy said. 'It's a giant tooth!'

'I think it's lunch-time,' Tania said. 'Let's go home now.'

'Yes, let's go home,' Troy agreed.

From the house they watched the beach. They could see the tooth, gleaming in the sun. Nobody came near it.

'You know, Troy,' Tania said. 'We could just go and see if it *is* writing.'

'That's what I've been thinking,' Troy agreed.

The letters were very big. Tania walked round them while Troy read them out.

dear looters this is my first please leave me

'If that's his tooth,' Tania said, 'how big would he be?'

'Very big,' Troy said. 'Humungous!'

'If it's his first tooth,' Tania went on, 'then he's only a little giant. Think how humungous his family must be.'

'I'd rather not think!' Troy said faintly. 'I'd rather go home. I definitely do not want to meet a humungous giant family on the beach. Expecially not just before Christmas.'

Tania ran after him. 'But, Troy, if his tooth's still there when he comes back, he'll think the tooth fairy isn't real.'

'It's none of our business,' Troy said. 'Anyway the tooth fairy isn't real.'

'Well, I think she's real,' Tania muttered. Her tooth was much looser.

Troy walked on.

'We could keep the tooth then,' Tania called after him. 'We could take the tooth away and bring him back some fairy gold. Oh, do let's do that, Troy!'

Troy turned and came back. 'I bet no one else has ever had a giant's tooth before! I bet it's really, really lucky!'

He grabbed Tania's hand and began to jump up and down with excitement. 'Let's go home and see what sort of fairy gold we can find,' he shouted.

'Wait, wait. We must make the bed first,' Tania said.

They tidied up the bed and gave it fresh seagrass sheets and then they picked up the tooth between them and carried it home.

Morris Lurie

THE TWENTY-SEVENTH ANNUAL AFRICAN HIPPOPOTAMUS RACE

ILLUSTRATED BY ELIZABETH HONEY

'I think you've got the makings of a champion,' says Edward's grandfather, but is Edward fast enough to win the greatest race along the mighty Zamboola River?

W HEN Edward had been measured, his grandfather told him to put his clothes back on again, and to hurry, because there were still things to do.

'Oh, dear!' said Edward's grandfather. 'It's nearly eleven o'clock. That's when the numbers are given out. Hurry, Edward. No time to lose!'

'My goodness!' said Edward's father. 'I'd forgotten all about the numbers.'

'What numbers?' Edward asked.

'Well,' said Edward's grandfather. 'When you get a lot of

hippopotamuses in the water at the same time, it's difficult to tell one from the other. And during a race, it's important to know which hippopotamus is which. Your school friends, for instance, will be on the look-out for you, and unless you have a number, they won't know which one is you.'

'Humphrey and Tad, William and Jeffrey, Benjamin and Luke!' cried Edward. 'Gosh! I'd forgotten all about them. I must go and find them.'

'You can,' said Edward's grandfather, 'when you've got your number. Up these steps. Here we are.'

Now Edward found himself standing on the *Official Numbers Given Here* platform. And just in time, too. It was eleven o'clock.

'Join the queue,' said Edward's grandfather, 'and when you've got your number, come back here. We'll be waiting for you.'

'Eighty-four Official Entrants!' thought Edward. 'Gosh! Will there be room in the river for all of us?'

'Nervous?' said a voice.

Edward turned around (he had been facing the wrong way, looking about) and saw that the Official Entrant just ahead of him in the queue was speaking to him.

'Gosh, yes!' said Edward.

'Me, too,' said the hippopotamus. 'My name's Barney. What's yours?'

'Edward,' said Edward.

'Pleased to meet you,' said Barney, offering his hand. 'Wow! Have you ever seen a crowd like this before? My stomach is full of the jitters!'

'Mine too!' said Edward, delighted to hear that someone else felt the way he did.

'Have you ever been to an Annual African Hippopotamus Race before?' asked Barney. 'I mean, even as a spectator?'

'No, I haven't,' said Edward. 'This is the first time.'

'Numbers are now being drawn!' called a voice.

'Gosh!' said Edward.

The queue started to move slowly forward, but what was at the end of it Edward didn't know. It was impossible to see, because there were so many hippopotamuses about.

'Do you think you'll win the race this afternoon?' Barney asked him.

'Gosh,' said Edward, 'I don't know. I haven't really thought about winning. I'm just going to swim as well as I can. Do you think you'll win, Barney?'

'Me?' said Barney. 'I don't know. Everyone in our neighbourhood says I'm a fast swimmer, but I don't really know. I'm just going to do my best, too.'

'I've been training for months and months,' said Edward.

'Me too,' said Barney.

'My grandfather has been training me,' said Edward. 'He was in the Fourth Annual African Hippopotamus Race. He came third.'

'My uncle trained me,' said Barney. 'He was in the Sixth Annual African Hippopotamus Race.'

The queue was moving along nicely, but there was still some way to go to where the numbers were being given out. Edward still couldn't see what was happening.

Suddenly, down below, there was a great noise.

'*Honk! Honk!*' Edward heard. 'Make way! Make way for the Mighty Sebastian! Make way! Make way!'

There came into view, travelling fast, a sleek, low, shiny, bright red sports car, with flashing silver wheels, and behind the steering wheel sat a huge hippopotamus.

He was the biggest hippopotamus Edward had ever seen, almost black in colour, with bright white teeth fixed in a hard grin. He was wearing a bright red jacket and a vivid green tie and white driving gloves, and, as Edward and Barney watched, he drove right up to the *Official Numbers Given Here* platform, brought his sleek red sports car to a sudden stop with a squeal of brakes, and then, with an easy swaggering air, climbed out of the seat. 'Who is that?' Edward whispered to Barney.

'I don't know,' Barney whispered back. 'Isn't he *huge*?'

'I'm the Mighty Sebastian!' announced the huge, dark hippopotamus, coming up the steps, two at a time, onto the platform. 'My name is Sebastian, and I mean to win this race! I'm the best and strongest and fastest hippopotamus in all Africa, and the race will be mine!'

'He's an Official Entrant,' Edward whispered to Barney.

Just then, an Official hippopotamus in a white coat came up.

'Are you an Official Entrant?' he asked Sebastian.

'What if I am?' said Sebastian.

'If you want a number,' said the Official hippopotamus, 'you'll have to join the end of the queue.'

'Sebastian doesn't queue for anything!' bellowed the huge, dark hippopotamus.

'Well,' said the Official hippopotamus, 'if you don't get in the queue, you won't get a number. And if you don't get a number, then you can't compete in the race.'

'Who says?' said Sebastian.

'I do,' said the Official. 'It might interest you to know that I'm the winner of last year's Annual African Hippopotamus Boxing and Wrestling Competition.'

'Oh,' mumbled Sebastian, and started to go off to the end of the queue, but just before going, he turned around, pounded his chest, and shouted, 'The Mighty Sebastian will win!'

'Isn't he a boaster?' whispered Edward.

'Even so,' said Barney, 'he *is* the biggest hippopotamus I have ever seen.'

'Move along, please!' called a voice. Both Edward and Barney quickly moved up.

They were near the front of the queue now, and at last Edward could see what was going on.

Right at the front of the queue stood a big wooden barrel, with an Official hippopotamus in a white coat standing next to it. As each Official Entrant came up, the Official hippopotamus dipped a big wooden spoon into the barrel and brought out a tiny white marble, which had a number on it, and handed it to the Official Entrant.

'Gosh!' said Edward. 'The numbers are tiny! No one will be able to see them when we're all in the river!'

'Next!' cried the Official hippopotamus in the white coat.

'Oh, that's me,' said Barney, stepping up to the barrel.

'Here we are,' said the Official to Barney, dipping the wooden

spoon into the big barrel. 'Number 51! Next!'

Now it was Edward's turn to get a number. Into the barrel went the spoon. Then out it came, bearing a small white marble.

'Number 65!' cried the Official, and handed the marble to Edward. 'Next, please!'

'This way,' said a voice, and Edward saw yet another Official hippopotamus waving him forward.

'Get your singlet here,' said the Official. 'Have your marble ready.'

'My singlet?' said Edward.

'This way,' said the Official, and then Edward saw a long table, and on it a pile of bright white singlets, each with a huge number on the back of it.

'Name and number, please,' said the Official.

'Um . . . Edward,' said Edward. 'Number 65.'

He gave his marble to the Official, who wrote it down in a book, together with Edward's name. Then he went to the pile of singlets, and brought out a bright white singlet with a big black number 65 on it.

'Try it on for size,' said the Official. 'Next please!'

The singlet was a perfect fit. Edward turned around and looked over his shoulder, to see how he looked at the back, and there was the number 65, plainly visible, for all to see. Edward felt very happy indeed to be wearing his singlet.

'It looks marvellous on you,' said Barney, who was standing nearby. 'How's mine?'

'Perfect,' said Edward. 'You look wonderful in it. I'm leaving mine on for my grandfather and my father to see. They're waiting for me. I'd better hurry.'

'See you at the race,' said Barney. 'Good luck.'

'Good luck,' said Edward, and shook Barney's hand, and then off he ran.

But just as he was running to find them, who should he bump into but Sebastian, who was still in the queue, waiting for his number.

'Watch where you're going,' grumbled Sebastian.

'I'm sorry,' said Edward. 'I didn't mean to bump into you.'

'You've got your number, I see,' said Sebastian, staring down at Edward. 'Well, if you want some advice, you'll take it off this minute and forget all about the race. You haven't got a chance, little hippopotamus! I'm going to win this race. The Mighty Sebastian! That's me! Ha ha ha!'

And with the Mighty Sebastian's laugh ringing in his ears, Edward ran off to find his grandfather and his father.

May Gibbs

SNUGGLEPOT AND CUDDLEPIE

ILLUSTRATED BY THE AUTHOR

Poor little Ragged Blossom discovers that Mrs Snake and the wicked Banksia men have evil plans. Can she save Snugglepot and Cuddlepie?

'THEY'LL be at the Lilly Pilly Pictures tomorrow; the Lizard will be outside. We must steal the Nuts and keep them till the Lizard comes to look for them, then we'll only give them up in exchange for him.'

'Aha!' said Mrs Snake's voice, 'that'll get him, the monster! How I hate him!'

'We'll starve those fat Nuts,' said one angry voice.

'Do 'em good,' said another horrible voice.

'And we'll kill the ugly Lizard they're so fond of,' said Mrs Snake's awful voice.

When Blossom heard these terrible things her hair stood straight up with fright. It was very cold in the passage, and, before she could stop it, Blossom sneezed. Mrs Snake darted to the door,

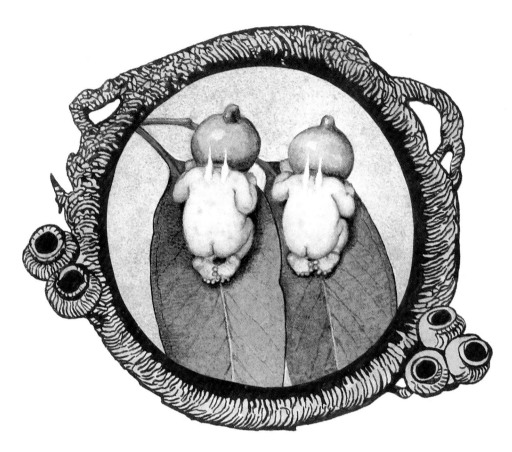

and was so astonished to see Blossom that she stood still, staring. Little Blossom sank trembling to the ground, her hands in the dust. Suddenly she thought of something. Like a flash she dashed two handfuls of dust into Mrs Snake's eyes, then jumped up and ran. It was uphill, but she ran. She was breathless, but she ran and ran. Her knees were giving way, but still she ran. She could hear them coming. Faster she ran, until at last she came to the top and fell out upon the moss.

They were coming! they were close behind! Blossom had just strength enough to crawl under a dead gum leaf and lie there as still as the moss. Several Banksia men came hurrying out of the hole.

'She's not out here,' said one.

'She must have hidden in the passage,' said another.

'Perhaps she's under that leaf,' said a third.

Blossom nearly jumped, but held her breath.

'What was that?' said one.

'It's Mrs Snake; she must have found her. Come on.' Then they all went in again, and Blossom heard them running and shouting down under the ground.

Worn out with excitement and running, Little Blossom sank into a long sleep. She was awakened by the heavy tread of a big Grey Possum on his rounds. (They are the policemen at night time because they can see in the dark.)

'Sh! Sh! What are you doing?' he asked, and Ragged Blossom told him everything.

'I'll watch the door while you go and warn the Nuts,' said he. 'I'd go with you only it's getting light; I'll soon have to go to bed.'

'Yes, it is,' said Blossom, 'I can hear the Ants taking round the Aphis milk.' So she hurried away.

It was nearly sunrise by the time she reached the city. Already it was getting warm, and the air was full of nice noises and sweet scents; the streets were crowded; busy Ants were running about everywhere; Beetle carts were labouring along; gay Nuts and fresh Blossoms were walking and chatting; Woodcutters were at work in the dark, everyone seemed busy and happy.

Poor Little Blossom was worried and sad. Who would listen to her story? She was so little and ragged. She must do something all by herself, but what could she do? She thought very hard, and soon a plan came to her.

She looked into lots of backyards till she saw a long spiderweb clothes line; and, as it was not washing-day, she borrowed it. Then she hurried along to the Lilly Pilly Picture Palace.

Tears fell as she thought of her beautiful ticket; but she was not a cry-baby, so she wiped away her tears and got to work.

First she climbed right up onto the top of the high building. It took a long time. Then she made a hole in the roof and tied one end of the rope firmly to a beam. No one noticed her, she was only like a fly on the roof. It was terrible to have to wait so long, but at last the people came. From her high perch she watched them crowd in; and at last, looking through the hole in the roof, she saw Snugglepot and Cuddlepie. There they were almost underneath her, near the wall. It was nearly time for the show to begin.

Kind old Mr Lizard was dozing out in the sun; and, behind him, in the deep shadows, she could see the glistening, wicked eyes of Mrs Snake and the bushy heads of the bad Banksia men.

Little Blossom longed to call to Mr Lizard and wake him; but she knew that would only warn the wicked ones, and they would then go away and make another plot; so she kept still and waited.

Presently the lights went out, and now was the time. A wonderful picture was showing. It was the Funny Nut, and every one was screaming with laughter. This was the very moment. Quickly she let down the rope till it hung just above the heads of Snugglepot and Cuddlepie; then she slid down beside Snugglepot. 'Hush!' she whispered, 'please let me see the pictures instead of you. I've never seen any; please do!'

Snugglepot and Cuddlepie were most astonished, but they had good bush manners, so Snugglepot only said, 'Of course, you take my place and I'll go out.'

'No, let me,' whispered Cuddlepie.

'No, I will,' answered Snugglepot, and he began to climb the rope. Cuddlepie followed, to argue with him, and they went up higher and higher still, saying, 'I want to go' – 'No, I will', and all the time the people were shouting with laughter at the picture and didn't see or hear them.

Little Ragged Blossom looked up; Snugglepot and Cuddlepie were safely out on the roof. She wanted to follow, but was too frightened.

Through the darkness she saw the wicked eyes of a Banksia man looking at her. Then something dashed in, grabbed her by the legs, dragged her out of the seat, hoisted her over the heads of the people and out of the Picture Show, all in a moment, faster than it can be told.

A hand was over her mouth, so she couldn't scream. She was carried along at a great speed, then she heard shouting and a great noise of people racing after them. 'Stop them! Stop them!' they were calling. At last they came to a steep hill.

'Throw her down,' hissed Mrs Snake.

'Not me,' panted the angry Banksia man.

Then quite suddenly they all seemed to fall down a big hole, and they rolled and rolled till they came to the bottom, and lay there panting.

'Thank goodness we're home,' said Mrs Snake, as soon as she got her breath again. 'Tie her up, and come and get something to

drink.' But Little Blossom couldn't run now, she lay quite still and cold.

'Never mind her, she's dead,' said a Banksia man.

'We'll get into trouble if she is,' said another.

'Pooh! She's only a little stray; no one will miss her', and so saying, Mrs Snake and the wicked Banksia men went away.

It was late in the afternoon, and Snugglepot and Cuddlepie and Mr Lizard were chewing wattle gum and resting by the road-side.

'How did you get up there on the roof?' asked Mr Lizard. Snugglepot told him.

'Why!' exclaimed Mr Lizard, 'she must have known the plot and was trying to save you.'

'Poor kind little Blossom,' said Snugglepot, 'if only we could find her!'

'Let's ask this tramp if he's seen them,' said Cuddlepie, as a tramp came hobbling along the road.

'Well, yes,' he said, rubbing his bushy beard, 'I seen some nasty-lookin' folk runnin' away with a little girl. They went in that direction. I heard 'em say they was goin' to the Gum Inn.'

'The Gum Inn,' shouted Mr Lizard. 'Jump on, we'll soon have them!'

As they galloped away, the old tramp threw back his head and laughed. He wasn't a tramp at all, but one of the wicked Banksia men disguised in a paperbark cloak. He hurried back to Mrs Snake.

'It's all right,' he said, 'I've sent them to the Gum Inn. If we hurry by the underground passage we'll get there first.'

'Good man,' said Mrs Snake.

Little Blossom, lying still, heard all that was said.

'What shall we do with her?' asked the Banksia men.

'Take her as far as the dungeon and throw her in. She's dead, or if not she soon will be,' said wicked Mrs Snake.

'Right-o,' said all the bad men.

So they picked up little Blossom and all started off. Blossom pretended to be dead, and, when they left her in the dungeon, lay still long after they had gone and their steps had died away. As she lay there, afraid to move, she heard a scratching noise quite near, and presently, in the dim light of the cave, she saw the earth and stones moving. Then a big hand came out of the earth, then another hand, then a face and two big eyes.

'Who are you?' said the face.

'I'm only little Ragged Blossom,' said the poor little thing. 'Please, don't kill me, please don't.'

'Are you a friend of Mrs Snake?' asked the face.

'No, I hate her,' said Ragged Blossom, who was always truthful.

'So do I,' said the face, and then the earth and stones heaved and out stepped a big Frog. He was very thin and pale, and seemed weak.

'Don't be afraid of me,' he said kindly; and he patted Blossom so gently that she burst into tears and told him all the story about Mrs Snake trying to catch Snugglepot and Cuddlepie, and how she meant to kill poor Mr Lizard. When the Frog heard this he grew very angry.

'Now is our chance to escape,' he said; 'they have left the door of the dungeon open. Come, I know the way to the river. Quick! I'll carry you;' and the big Frog carried little Blossom till they came to a cave with a lake in it.

'Shut your eyes and hold on to me, and don't be afraid,' said the Frog, and then he dived into the water and swam under, and came out into the diving-pool. Mr Frog clambered out and looked round. No one was about.

'Come,' said he, shaking the water off little Blossom. 'Quickly! There's no time to lose.'

He hurried down the bed of the creek till they came to a big river. Here, under the rushes, lay a little boat. They jumped in. He pushed out into the stream and away they went, twirling and bobbing along with the current. After rushing down the stream at a great rate for some time, Mr Frog guided the little boat into a quiet pool and pushed her on to the bank.

'Where are we?' asked Blossom.

'In the garden of the Gum Inn,' he answered.

'Come on! Hurry! or we shall be too late,' he cried; and, as he spoke, a loud shriek filled the air; then shouts and more shrieks. Mr Frog turned pale, and Blossom's knees shook so that she could scarcely run. All the time, as they hurried up through the garden, they could hear the terrible noise.

'They must be killing . . .' began Blossom.

'Don't talk; hurry!' said the Frog; and he went so fast that she could scarcely keep him in sight. At the top of the garden was a little gateway leading into the road. They opened the gate and looked out.

What they saw made them stand rooted to the spot with horror. There, in front of the Inn, riding on the Lizard, were Snugglepot and Cuddlepie. Mr Lizard was reared up on his hind legs, and there, almost upon them, was the huge shining body of Mrs Snake. Her head was raised to strike; but now a wonderful thing happened.

High above Mrs Snake swung the sign of the Gum Inn, and on it sat a Nut painting it, who, seeing what was about to happen, sprang from the sign right upon the neck of Mrs Snake, and, with arms and legs about her throat, held her fast.

Her great tail whipped the road. Everyone screamed. The Lizard dashed upon her, and held her down. Snugglepot and Cuddlepie shouted to some men who all rushed upon her. More men came running down the road, and men from the Inn. Mr Frog came to himself and leapt upon her. With so many against her, Mrs Snake saw that her end had come. She called, 'Help! Friends, help!' But the cowardly Banksia men had fled, and were now far away.

So Mrs Snake was tied head and tail till she couldn't move, and her wicked head was knocked off. A great shout went up, for she was very wicked and deserved to die, and everyone was glad.

INDEX OF AUTHORS

ACKNOWLEDGEMENTS

The publisher gratefully acknowledges the following for permission to reproduce copyright stories in this book.

Extract from *Little Brother* by Allan Baillie, first published by Blackie & Son Ltd, l985, text copyright © Allan Baillie, l985, and colour plate from the cover of the Puffin edition copyright © Jane Tanner, 1995, reprinted from the Puffin edition with permission of Penguin Books Australia Ltd.

The Wolf by Margaret Barbalet, illustrated by Jane Tanner, first published by Penguin Books Australia Ltd, l991, text copyright © Margaret Barbalet, 1991, illustrations copyright © Jane Tanner, 1991, reprinted with permission of Penguin Books Australia Ltd.

Extract from *The Sign of the Seahorse* by Graeme Base, first published byPenguin Books Australia Ltd, l992, text and illustrations copyright © Doublebase Pty Ltd, l992, reprinted with permission of Penguin Books Australia Ltd.

Extract from *Tangara* by Nan Chauncy, first published by Oxford University Press, London, l960, text copyright © Nan Chauncy, l960, and colour plate from the cover of the Puffin edition copyright © David Legge, 1991, reprinted from the Puffin edition with permission of Penguin Books Australia Ltd.

Extract from *A Fortunate Life* by A.B. Facey, first published by Fremantle Arts Centre Press, l981, text copyright © Albert B. Facey, l981, and colour plate from the cover of the Puffin edition copyright © Anne Spudvilas, 1995, reprinted from the edition prepared by the editors of Readers Digest Condensed Books with permission of Penguin Books Australia Ltd.

'The Railway Historical Steam Weekend' and 'A Short, Summery Thin, Thong Song' from *Wry Rhymes for Troublesome Times* by Max Fatchen, illustrated by Michael Atchison, first published by Kestrel Books, l983, text copyright © Max Fatchen, l983, illustrations copyright © Michael Atchison, 1983, reprinted with permission of Penguin Books Ltd, UK.

'No Naughty Boys, Please', 'Call that a Party?' and 'The Love Letter' from *I Hate Fridays* by Rachel Flynn, illustrated by Craig Smith, first published by Penguin Books Australia Ltd, l990, text copyright © Rachel Flynn, l990, illustrations copyright © Craig Smith, l990, and colour plate from the cover of the Puffin edition copyright © Craig Smith, 1990, reprinted with permission of Penguin Books Australia Ltd.

Extract from *Snugglepot and Cuddlepie* written and illustrated by May Gibbs, first published by Angus & Robertson Publishers, l940, copyright © The Spastic Centre of NSW and The Northcott Society, 1940, reprinted from the Angus & Robertson Classic Edition, l990, with permission of HarperCollins*Publishers*

Extract from *Me and Mary Kangaroo* by Kevin Gilbert, with photographs by Eleanor Williams, first published by Penguin Books Australia Ltd, 1994, text copyright © Kevin Gilbert, l994, illustrations copyright © Kevin Gilbert and Eleanor Williams, l994, photographs copyright © Eleanor Williams, l994, and colour plate by Eleanor Williams from the cover of the Viking edition, hand-coloured by Mark Sofilas, copyright © Eleanor Williams, reprinted with permission of Penguin Books Australia Ltd.